"Yes," was all Shelley said. She looked so alone and vulnerable that he wanted to reach across the table and grab her hand. But he hung on to his mug because that was a lot safer than touching her.

"So, what brings you here?" While she'd been sleeping, he'd let his imagination run wild. She was in trouble. He knew that much. But after five years, why come to him?

Suddenly she looked as if she wanted to cry—and as if she wasn't going to give in to tears.

"My son, Trevor, has been kidnapped," she blurted. "I think you're the only one who can help me find him."

Although the words reached his ears, he never would have expected them. "I didn't know you'd gotten married."

"I didn't. He's four years old, Matt. And he's your son, too."

REBECCA YORK

RUTH GLICK WRITING AS REBECCA YORK

POWERHOUSE

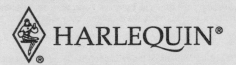

HARLEQUIN®

TORONTO • NEW YORK • LONDON
AMSTERDAM • PARIS • SYDNEY • HAMBURG
STOCKHOLM • ATHENS • TOKYO • MILAN • MADRID
PRAGUE • WARSAW • BUDAPEST • AUCKLAND

Special thanks and acknowledgment to Rebecca York for her contribution to the Maximum Men series.

Recycling programs
for this product may
not exist in your area.

ISBN-13: 978-0-373-69454-9

POWERHOUSE

www.eHarlequin.com

Printed in U.S.A.

ABOUT THE AUTHOR

Award-winning, bestselling novelist Ruth Glick, who writes as Rebecca York, is an author of more than one hundred books, including her popular 43 Light Street series for Harlequin Intrigue. Ruth says she has the best job in the world. Not only does she get paid for telling stories, she's also the author of twelve cookbooks. Ruth and her husband, Norman, travel frequently, researching locales for her novels and searching out new dishes for her cookbooks.

Books by Rebecca York

Don't miss any of our special offers. Write to us at the following address for information on our newest releases.

Harlequin Reader Service
U.S.: 3010 Walden Ave., P.O. Box 1325, Buffalo, NY 14269
Canadian: P.O. Box 609, Fort Erie, Ont. L2A 5X3

CAST OF CHARACTERS

Matt Whitlock—Was he a powerhouse or a danger to himself and others?

Shelley Young—She walked away from Matt five years ago. Now she was desperate for his help rescuing her son.

Trevor Young—Would he ever see his mom again?

Blue—Why had he kidnapped Trevor?

Bobby Savage and Don Campbell—What did they want with Matt and Shelley?

Perry Owens—Was the FBI agent going to help find Trevor?

Jack Maddox and Claudia Reynolds—Were they being straight with Matt and Shelley?

Ed Janey—Would the ranch foreman back up Matt's crazy story?

Chapter One

Desperation kept Shelley Young plowing through the blinding snow. Of course, she'd seen the weather forecast, but she'd left Boulder anyway, praying that she'd outrun the storm as she headed down Route 76 toward Yuma. In other words, the middle of nowhere. A part of Colorado she'd avoided since she'd broken up with Matt Whitlock five years ago. She'd been in love with him, but she'd finally figured out that he couldn't give her the things she wanted most—marriage and children. Walking away from him had wrenched her heart, but she'd made a clean break, moving her accounting business a hundred and forty miles away to Boulder, where she'd been living ever since.

"It's all for the best," her mom would have said. For a while Shelley had believed it, but she'd been wrong. Because now she was back—to beg Matt Whitlock for help. Only she'd gotten caught in a storm that blanked out every recognizable feature of the flat eastern Colorado landscape.

This was an area of sudden, violent weather. Thunderstorms in the summer and snowstorms in the winter.

Like now. But what did she expect? In the time it took to read a couple of heart-stopping sentences, her life had fallen to pieces—and plowing through the blinding snow was just one more trial she had to get through to put it back together.

If she *could* put it back together.

Although the windshield wipers swept back and forth in front of her, they didn't help much. If only she'd noted the odometer reading when she'd left Boulder, she'd have a better idea where she was, but she'd been too focused on getting here to check anything on the dashboard besides the gas gauge.

She almost missed the turn-off for the Silver Stallion Ranch, but from the corner of her eye, she caught sight of the familiar metal archway above the stone gateposts.

Skidding as she applied the brakes, she peered up the narrow drive that led to the ranch complex. There were no tire tracks, which meant no one had been up or down the access road since the storm had started.

Her heart gave a painful lurch. After she'd come so far, was Matt away? Or was he just holed up in the ranch house, waiting out the bad weather?

Clamping her hands onto the wheel, she turned in between the gateposts and started up the lane. Once this had been familiar territory. Now she might as well be traveling through an arctic wasteland.

When the car skidded on hidden ice, she cautiously tapped the brake, wondering when Matt had last plowed the drive. It felt as if he hadn't spread a fresh layer of gravel since she'd been here.

What did the lack of upkeep mean? Was he low on funds? Or had he withdrawn even more into the shell she'd watched him building around himself?

With a sick feeling, she looked back over her shoulder, questioning her decision to come here in the first place.

But she'd had nowhere else to turn, and retracing her path would be tricky.

She managed to drive perhaps another fifty yards before the car hit an obstruction hidden in the snow. When she tried to back up, she fishtailed into the ditch at the side of the road.

If she'd been a man, she would have responded with a string of curses, but she made do with one ladylike "damn."

She was good at keeping her temper under control. Maybe that was part of her problem. She was too polite to make a fuss, which was one of the reasons she hadn't contacted Matt five years ago when...

She took her bottom lip between her teeth, unwilling to finish the thought. She'd have to get to that soon enough.

Her cell phone was in her purse, but when she pulled it out, she got another nasty surprise. Usually she charged it overnight, but that was one more detail she'd neglected in the past few days. Now the battery was dead as a tree stump.

"Damn!"

She'd just have to walk the rest of the way to the ranch house.

With a sigh, she looked in the back seat. Her overnight bag was there, but carrying it through the snow was out of the question. After slinging the strap of her purse across her chest, she yanked her wool hat down more firmly over her dark hair, pulled her scarf up over her nose and climbed out of the car.

Immediately, the wind whipped against her slender frame, making her grab the car door to brace herself. When she felt steady on her feet, she raised her arm to shield her eyes from the stinging flakes and started plodding up the drive, glad that at least the snow wasn't higher than the top of her boots.

UP AT THE ranch house, Matt Whitlock shut off the alarm that had warned him that someone was on the road to the main complex. Someone he obviously wasn't expecting.

Now who would be out in a storm like this?

A traveler who needed to take shelter from the driving snow? Or someone using the weather as an excuse to sneak up on him?

He made a snorting sound. There was a time in his life when

he would have considered that last thought over-the-top paranoid. From bitter experience, he'd learned that paranoia could be entirely justified.

He turned toward the window, looking out at the sea of white. From here, he couldn't even see the bunkhouse where his one remaining hand, Ed Janey, lived. It was tempting to stay inside and let the trespasser make the next move. Still, whoever was out there could be in trouble if he hadn't figured on a sudden storm. If Matt didn't want to find a frozen body in the road tomorrow morning, he'd better go out and have a look.

Or maybe he'd encounter a deer looking for shelter.

With a sense of resignation, he made his way to the mudroom that he used more than the front entrance of the ranch house.

Along one wall was a bench where he sat down to lace up sturdy boots. Next, he strapped on a holster and pulled his Sig Sauer from the gun cabinet. Not the weapon of choice for most ranchers, but it seemed more useful than a rifle under the circumstances. After clicking in a magazine, he holstered the weapon, then took a down coat and a broad-brimmed hat from pegs on the wall. Prepared for the storm—and for trouble— he stepped out of the house into the storm.

A stinging blast of snow hit him in the face, and he shook his head. The smart thing would be to go back inside, but he was out here now, and he might as well find out who the devil was stupid enough to be traveling on a February day like this.

"OH, WHEN the saints come marching in," Shelley sang as she struggled up the road toward the ranch.

Belting out the lively hymn helped keep her mind off her precarious situation, but she gave up when she realized she needed all her energy just to keep plowing through the snow. In the distance, she thought she saw a light, but it might simply be a mirage.

Born and bred in Colorado, she was used to extremes of weather, but it had been a long time since she'd gone out in a storm like this. If she'd been thinking about her own safety, she would have waited a couple of days before heading for Matt's ranch, but her problem had been too urgent to put off. And it hadn't been something she could talk about over the phone.

Now she was wondering if she had a chance of making it to the house.

Her foot collided with yet another hidden obstruction, and she almost went down—but managed to stay on her feet by windmilling her arms.

After taking a moment to catch her breath, she started forward again. As the light faded, the temperature dropped, and numbing cold began to penetrate her coat.

Tears blurred her vision, but she blinked them away. If she let herself get worked up, she was going to start screaming— or sobbing, and that wasn't going to do her any good.

Instead, she kept putting one foot in front of the other as she lowered her head against the wind and followed the road as best she could toward the ranch complex.

The wind kicked up, blowing the snow into drifts that blocked her way. She judged that she had covered about half the distance between the car and the house when she blundered off the driveway and into the ditch—which was piled with snow.

For a long moment, she lay where she was—panting. Then she forced herself up because she knew that if she stayed where she was, she'd end up freezing to death. Lips set in a grim line, she scrambled back onto the road, but now her steps were slower, and she knew she was in serious danger of going down again.

MATT WAS several hundred yards from the house when he saw something through a curtain of falling snow. A person, struggling up the driveway that led to the ranch yard.

"This way," he called out.

There was no response, and he knew the wind had drowned out the sound of his voice. As he watched, the guy pitched over into a snowdrift and lay still.

Matt picked up his pace. The damn fool was in trouble— whoever it was.

"Just stay there. I'm coming," he called out, then laughed harshly at himself. It didn't look like the interloper was going anywhere under his own power.

Matt tramped onward through the blizzard, finally reaching the guy, who had fallen in the snow and didn't have the strength to get up.

Squatting down, he turned the man over and pulled down the scarf that covered his face.

When large green eyes blinked open, he made a strangled sound.

"Shelley?"

"Matt…" she gasped out as she focused on his face. "Thank God."

"What are you doing here?"

She blinked, and her lips moved, but she apparently didn't have the strength to answer.

"Come on." He helped her to her feet and slung his arm around her waist, holding her erect.

"Can you walk?"

"I…think so."

He was cursing himself for not bringing a four-wheeler down the road, but he'd been too intent on sneaking up on the intruder. Now he was stuck walking Shelley back to the house.

Holding her firmly against his side, he turned and retraced his steps, following his own trail through the snow.

It was still falling like a son of a bitch, and it was hard to see where he was going. But he pushed his surprise guest onward as fast as he could make her walk because he knew he had to get her out of the cold and wind as soon as possible.

As he held her upright, images from the past assaulted him—starting with a very nervous Shelley Young, just out of college, interviewing for the job of his accountant. She'd worn her brown hair longer then. He skipped a few months and saw himself and Shelley in his office, going over the computer files. The two of them at the breakfast table. Walking hand and hand along the creek. Down by the corral—feeding carrots to the horses.

He tried to keep one more vivid picture out of his mind—him and Shelley naked in bed, in each other's arms, clinging desperately together because they both sensed that the relationship was never going to work out, and neither of them was willing to admit it.

He squeezed his eyes closed, struggling against that last image and against his own reaction. If he was smart, he would put her into a four-wheel SUV and drive her back to Boulder, where she was living now.

But he couldn't do it. She must have come here for a reason, and he needed to find out what it was. Still, he knew he had his own reasons for bringing her inside.

If he could have her here for just a little while, maybe that would be enough to last him another five lonely years.

When they finally reached the house, he muttered a prayer of thanks as he helped her through the door. Once they were in the warmth of the house, he sat her down on the bench in the mudroom and pulled off her boots, coat and purse.

"Matt?"

"It's okay. What are you doing here?"

She shook her head, and he could tell she wasn't exactly with it.

After tossing his own coat on the floor and pulling off his boots, he picked Shelley up in his arms and carried her through the kitchen, then down the hall to the room where he had slept when he was a kid.

He'd long ago moved into the master bedroom where he had more space to spread out, but he'd kept this room in case he needed it. Yeah, sure. For what?

Well, at least he didn't have to put Shelley in his bed. That was something.

He propped her against his hip then pulled the covers aside and eased her onto the bed. When she was lying down, he reached for her feet. They were cold and wet, so he pulled her socks off and inspected her toes, which were red but not frost-bitten. When he found that the hems of her jeans were wet, he opened the snap at her waist, pulled down her zipper and dragged the pants down her legs.

"You're undressing me," she murmured, her lips curving in a silly grin.

"We need to get you warm and dry," he answered, peeling down her thermal underwear and discarding it along with her jeans, struggling to ignore his reaction to her slim legs, feminine thighs and the triangle of dark hair he could see through the thin fabric of her panties.

Luckily, her shirt was still dry, so he dragged the sheet and blanket over her, covering the tempting image of her lying in bed.

"You need to sleep."

"I need you."

Her arms whipped out and circled his neck, pulling him down so that he flopped on top of her.

"Shelley."

"I need you, Matt," she whispered, her voice quavery.

"For what? Why did you come here?"

She made a muffled sound.

When he lifted his head to gaze down at her, she still looked dazed and confused, and he knew he should climb off the bed and beat a retreat into the other room.

As he hesitated, she cupped the back of his head and

brought his mouth to hers, and he couldn't make himself pull away. When his lips touched down on hers, a jolt of sensation shot through him.

Somewhere in his mind, he knew none of this should be happening. He shouldn't be in a bed with her—holding her—for so many reasons.

Yet at this moment in time, none of the reasons mattered. The only thing his brain had room for was that she was lying in his embrace.

He broke the kiss and lifted his head. Her lips were parted now, her breath shallow, her eyes full of hope—and, he thought, pain.

"What is it?"

"Just be with me."

Unable to deny the invitation, he maneuvered to the side, gathering her close, and it was the most natural thing in the world to bring his mouth back to hers, nibbling, sliding, taking her lower lip into his mouth the way he'd always liked to do.

She tasted wonderful, as sweet as he remembered, but the best part was her response to him. The returned pressure of her lips against his and the way she moved restlessly on the bed fueled a hot, frantic burst of sensation inside him.

Not just him. He could feel needs zinging back and forth between them.

He was on top of the covers. She was underneath. He knew he should keep her warm, so he slipped off the bed—just long enough to pull the blanket and sheet aside and slide in next to her, so he could gather her close.

When she made a small sound of approval, he ran his hands up and down her back, then cupped her bottom, pulling her against the erection straining at the front of his jeans.

He had missed her so much. Needed her so much, and now here she was, right where he wanted her—warm and cozy with him in bed. He heard a sound well up in her throat. Or perhaps it was from his throat. He couldn't even be sure.

Her hands began to move too, roving restlessly over his back, his shoulders, pulling him closer.

They clung together, rocking slightly in the bed, as the kiss turned more urgent—more hungry—driving every thought from his mind but one. Against all reason, she had come back to him, and he must make love to her before she slipped away from him again.

Was this reality or a fantasy? He didn't know, and he didn't care. The taste and feel of Shelley Young was the only reality in his universe.

His mouth moved over hers, feasting on her, his tongue sliding along the rigid line of her teeth, then beyond.

It was all so familiar. So precious. It was as though they had never been apart, as though the past five years had never happened.

As he kissed her, he eased far enough away to slide one hand between them so that he could cup her breast and stroke his fingers over the tip. He remembered how sweetly she responded to him, how she gave him as much as he took. And when he reached under her sweater to unhook her bra, she made a small sound of approval, then sighed in pleasure as he took her nipples between his thumbs and fingers, twisting and pulling, doing the things he remembered that she liked.

"Shelley."

She answered with his name, and somehow that brought a dose of reality into the fantasy world he had created in the warmth of the bed.

"Oh, Shelley."

When he put some space between them, her eyes snapped open, questioning his.

"We can't do this," he said in a gritty voice.

"Why not?"

"Because I just brought you in out of the snow, and you're not in any condition to be making sexual decisions."

"Sexual decisions," she repeated.

"Get some rest. When you're ready, we'll talk about why you drove through a snowstorm to come here."

A look that was part desperation, part regret, part passion passed over her face, reflecting his own feelings with an aching intensity. He could take what he wanted. Right now.

And then what? He'd hate himself for a long time afterward.

Unwilling to prolong the moment, he climbed out of the bed and stood looking down at her.

"Matt?"

"Shelley, go to sleep," he said softly.

Her green eyes looked confused. "I...don't want to sleep. I have to talk to you."

"Not now. Go to sleep," he repeated. "For me."

She blinked. "Now?"

"Yes."

"All...right," she said in a barely audible voice.

As her eyes fluttered closed, he stood looking down at her, thankful that he could influence her decision, yet wondering how he was going to cope with having her in the house again. As soon as he'd taken her in his arms, all the need and longing he'd repressed for years had flared up. It was as though the two of them had never been apart.

He cursed softly under his breath, angry at his own weakness. He wanted to be angry with her, too. She'd come here unannounced and tempted him beyond endurance.

Why hadn't she just called him on the phone?

A shiver went through him. A phone call was a perfectly logical means of communication. Instead she'd driven here through a dangerous storm. Which led to the conclusion that she was afraid someone might be monitoring her calls. Or that she had some news that could only be said face-to-face. What could that be?

He took a step toward the bed and reached out, then stopped

himself before he could grab her arm and shake her awake again.

He had to talk to her, but his previous judgment had been correct. She needed to sleep—so she'd be in good enough shape to tell him the bad news straight up. Because he sensed that whatever she was going to say would be like a punch in the gut.

Chapter Two

Shelley moved restlessly on the bed. She didn't want to wake up, but she couldn't stay hiding here forever.

Hiding from what?

Deliberately, she opened her eyes and looked around the unfamiliar room.

Panic gripped her as she struggled to remember where she was. Then the past few terrible days came zinging back to her. And the past few hours—when she'd gotten into her car and started driving east—to Matt's ranch. Because she simply didn't know what else to do.

She'd turned in at the gate and gotten stuck in the snow and started walking to the ranch house. She'd still be out there if Matt hadn't come down the road and found her.

How had he even known she was on the ranch property?

She wasn't sure, but it was lucky for her that he had. He'd brought her back…and, oh Lord. They had ended up in a passionate clinch—under the covers. In this bed, and if he hadn't gotten up and walked away, they would have made love—just like that.

Which meant she'd been kidding herself for the past five years. She'd had the strength to walk away from Matt Whitlock because that was the only way to cut off the pain of their relationship, but she'd never gotten over him. And in a few minutes, she was going to have to tell him something that might make him hate her.

And after *that* she was going to beg for his help.

Would he understand her decision five years ago? Would he help her? Or would he order her out of the house? She hoped not until she could get her car out of the snowbank. And then what? She'd be right back where she'd started. In desperate trouble.

That thought made her swing her legs over the side of the bed. She had to get this over with. Now. Standing, she looked around. Her jeans and long johns were gone, and she remembered that Matt had pulled them off. Probably because they were wet from her falls into snowbanks.

In place of her discarded clothing were a pair of sweatpants and some thick socks enveloped by his familiar scent. The pants were too big for her slender five-foot-nine-inch frame, and the socks flopped around on her feet. His, she presumed. She pulled on the pants, then the socks. When she didn't see her purse, she had a moment of panic. Then she figured it was with her coat and boots in the mudroom. In the bathroom, she finger-combed her hair and splashed water on her face, then inspected her visage, wishing she had some lipstick. She didn't look great, but it would have to do. And she knew she was only stalling for time. Despite her earlier resolve, she was having a failure of nerve again.

She bought herself a few more moments by turning to the window. The storm had blown over, and the moon had risen, making a path of light along the snow-covered ground. Looking at her watch, she saw that she'd been asleep for a couple of hours.

Through the window she could see the familiar outline of the bunkhouse. Only one dim light burned over there. When she'd been here five years ago, the place had been blazing at night.

No more.

Where were the men who worked for Matt?

Well, that wasn't her concern, really.

Before she could think of some other excuse to stay in here, she pulled open the door and walked down the hall. Past the office where she and Matt had worked on his accounts together. Past the comfortable den where they'd watched DVDs and eaten popcorn in the evenings.

Sometimes they'd get a popular TV series and start watching the first season. Not once a week but two or three episodes a night if they were really hooked. She smiled at the memory as she continued through the empty dining room— and finally into the kitchen.

Matt was standing at the stove, his shoulders rigid, and she saw that every nerve in his body was crackling with tension. Obviously, he'd heard her coming, and he was wondering what the two of them were going to say to each other.

She'd set him on edge, and she wanted to whisper "sorry." But that wasn't a very good way to start off this confrontation.

Of course, there *was* no good way.

As she stopped in the doorway, he turned quickly, and she gave him a long look. She'd been too out of it to really see him earlier. Now she took in his dark, sun-streaked hair, the worried look in his blue eyes, and the tension around his strong jaw.

"How are you?" he asked.

"Okay. Thanks to you. How did you know I was out there?"

"I have an alarm system."

"You do?"

"Yeah. I knew somebody was on the road."

She nodded, wondering when he'd put that in. Her head jerked toward the bunkhouse. "Do your men bed down early?"

He kept his gaze fixed on her. "I'm not working the ranch. Only Ed Janey is over there."

"Why?"

"Ed's been here a long time. He doesn't have anywhere else to go."

She swallowed, trying to take it all in. It seemed a lot had changed in five years, and nobody had told her. But why would they?

"I mean—why aren't you working the ranch?"

"I made some good investments, and I pulled my money out before the stock market crashed. I'm living on that."

MATT WATCHED Shelley's reaction. She was probably trying to wrap her head around all the changes that had taken place since they'd seen each other last.

He didn't particularly want to explain his reasoning to her. It would be easier simply to send her away. Not in so many words—but to plant the idea in her head. The way he'd planted the idea of her going to sleep.

But she looked strung out, and not just from getting half frozen. She'd come here because something was badly wrong, and he had to find out what it was—and if there was some way he could help her.

The teakettle whistled, giving him an excuse to turn back to the stove. After lifting the kettle off the burner, he opened the cabinet and took down two packets of hot chocolate.

Still with his back to her, he poured the contents into two mugs, then stirred, stirring up memories as the scent of chocolate wafted toward him.

He and Shelley had sat in the evenings in front of the fire sipping hot chocolate. They'd talked about all sorts of things, and he'd felt so close to her. Well, as close as he could feel to anyone when he had a secret that he had to guard at all costs.

"That smells good."

"You always liked hot chocolate," he answered.

When she sat down at the table, he set the mugs between

them, careful not to touch her. Then he pulled out the chair opposite her and sat.

Neither one of them spoke.

For something to do, he took a sip of the hot liquid. She did the same, her hands wrapped around the crockery. It looked as though she was holding on for dear life.

He could barely taste the drink as he waited for her to tell him why she was here. She looked so alone and vulnerable that he wanted to reach across the table and grab her hand. But he hung on to his own mug because that was a lot safer than touching her.

Finally, when she didn't speak, he cleared his throat. "It's been a long time."

"Yes."

While she'd been sleeping, he'd let his imagination run wild. She was in trouble. He knew that much. And he'd turned over all the possibilities in his mind. Had her business crashed in the recession, and she needed money? Had a client asked her to do something illegal? Had she discovered someone was cooking the books at a company, and she didn't know what to do about it? Or was it something personal? He didn't even want to speculate on what that might be.

Forcing the issue, he finally asked, "What brings you here?"

Suddenly she looked as if she wanted to cry—and as if she wasn't going to give in to tears.

"You'll feel better when you tell me."

"I doubt it." She swallowed hard, then raised her head and met his gaze. "My son, Trevor, has been kidnapped," she blurted. "I think you're the only one who can help me find him."

Although the words reached his ears, they didn't really make sense. Maybe because, in a million years, he never would have expected them.

"Did I hear that right? You have a son, and he's been kidnapped?"

"Yes."

"Good Lord. I didn't know…I mean. You have a son?" he said again, totally confounded by the revelation. The obvious thought leaped into his mind, and he felt his stomach clench. "I didn't know you'd gotten married."

She continued to meet his gaze. "I'm not married. He's four years old, Matt. He's your son, too."

The shock and confusion was like a body blow, and for a moment he couldn't breathe. Shaking his head, he tried to clear his brain. He couldn't be hearing her correctly—could he? "I don't think I'm getting all of this quite right."

In a high, strained voice, she said, "I know I've shocked you. I didn't know how else to say it. Five years ago, I left you because you told me you didn't want to get married. And you didn't want children. Then I found out I was pregnant, and I wasn't going to come back and beg you to marry me. So I just…." She let go of the mug and flapped one arm. "I just went it alone."

He tried to imagine what she'd been through, what she was going through now.

"You're saying he's been kidnapped?" Matt said, his own voice turning rough. This was like a nightmare. An old nightmare coming back. Only she didn't know it yet.

"Yes."

He asked the next obvious question. "And the police and the FBI are looking for him?"

The scared, determined look on her face tore at his heart. "No! I can't go to them."

"You have to!"

"I can't!" she shouted, then lowered her voice. "Somebody picked him up at day care two days ago. A man, apparently. He made the teacher think he had my permission. But he left a note for me with her. It said that if I contacted the police or the FBI, they'd kill Trevor."

The revelation tipped her over the edge. It looked as if she'd been holding herself together with strapping tape. Suddenly, all pretense of composure evaporated. She began to cry in great gulping gasps, her shoulders shaking as the sobs racked her body.

Matt shot out of his chair, came around the table and hauled her up. When he wrapped his arms around her, she leaned into him. As he folded her close, he knew he needed to hold on to her as much as she needed to cling to him.

While he rocked her gently in his arms, he tried to process everything she'd just told him. It was too much to take in all at once, but he had to because the past was rushing back to body-slam him.

Shelley gulped, and he could feel her trying to pull herself together.

Now he was the one who was hanging on to composure by a thread.

"You have no idea who took him?" he asked.

"No," she whispered.

"And you have no idea what they want?"

"No."

"They didn't ask for money?"

"I'm telling you everything I know."

He stroked her back. "Okay. I believe you." Sucking in a breath, he let it out in a rush, knowing he was going to make this worse for her. For both of them.

"A long time ago, I was kidnapped," he said.

Her head jerked up, and she stared at him through brimming eyes. "What?"

He had turned the tables on her. Now she had to process what she was hearing.

"You were kidnapped?"

"Yes."

"You never told me about it!"

"It's not something I was prepared to talk about—with anyone." But now that he'd opened the subject, he knew she had a thousand questions, and he would do his best to answer them. He'd told her she'd feel better when she explained why she'd come. Strangely, he was discovering the truth of his own words. Despite the circumstances, it was a relief to stop lying. Well, lying by omission.

"How old were you?"

"Twelve." Before she could ask another question, he pressed ahead. "A couple of friends and I had gotten off the school bus. A white van stopped and somebody pulled me inside."

"Who?"

"I don't remember!"

"But you got away!" she whispered, and he knew she was grasping onto that fact. He was here. Somehow he'd escaped from his captors.

"I came back three months later. I don't have any memories of what happened to me while I was gone. The next thing I remember is wandering along the stream on the ranch."

"You were safe!"

"Yeah. But I made the decision never to have children. Never to put a child of my own in danger. Now I know I was right."

"Matt, what are you saying?" she gasped, obviously trying to put it all together.

"Shelley, it can't be a coincidence that I was kidnapped, and then Trevor. It's got to be related."

When she stared at him, stunned, he said, "I understand your confusion. Let's sit down where we'll be comfortable."

He led her down the hall to the den where they'd sat on so many evenings long ago. After seating her on the sofa, he crossed to the fireplace and removed the screen. Kneeling down, he struck a long match and lit the kindling under the dry logs in the grate, watching them flame up.

When she turned, he saw Shelley huddled on the cushions, staring at the fire as though the flames held the answer to their problems.

"I tried," he said. "I tried to keep it from happening again."

She nodded, and he knew he had to tell her the rest of it.

Still standing with his back to the fire, he said, "I may not remember what happened to me, but I know it changed me."

Lifting her gaze, she asked, "How?"

He swallowed, because as bad as the first part of his revelation had been, he was just getting to the worst part.

BIG BOYS don't cry. Trevor Young knew that, but it was hard to keep tears from leaking down his cheeks.

He was cold and hungry, and he wanted to go home. He wanted his mommy.

With a trembling hand, he swiped the tears away.

"Mommy," he whispered so that the man named Blue wouldn't hear him. "Mommy, please come get me out of here." He didn't think that she could hear him. But he couldn't stop himself from talking to her because it made him feel a little better.

He was in a cabin in the middle of a field—with trees all around the edges, except where the road cut through. He could look out the window, but he couldn't see any other houses. Maybe there were some behind the trees. Or maybe not.

He wanted to get away. But the window was locked. And so was the door. And sometimes Blue put a handcuff on Trevor like the police did on TV when they were taking the bad guys to the police station. The cuff was attached to a chain. And the chain was attached to the bed frame. So he couldn't move very far.

Only it was all backward now. The bad guy had the handcuffs. Not the police.

He lay curled on the bed, hugging his knees. When he heard the doorknob turn, he burrowed under the covers, wishing he could hide.

Footsteps crossed the wooden floor, and he knew Blue was looking down at him. If he pretended to be sleeping, would the man go away?

Instead, he pulled down the blanket, and Trevor couldn't stop himself from whimpering. "Please, let me go back to my mommy."

"Don't give me a hard time, kid."

"Why are you so mean?"

"It's my job."

"What kind of job is that?"

"Stop asking questions."

The hard look in the man's eyes made Trevor clamp his lips together.

Blue pulled his hand from behind his back, and Trevor saw that he was holding a hypodermic needle.

Trevor cringed away. The man had already given him some shots that hurt a lot. In his back. "Please, please don't do that to me again."

"Shut up. The sooner we do this, the sooner it will be over."

As the man grabbed his arm, Trevor started to cry.

SHELLEY STARED at the harsh lines of Matt's face. The way he said that being kidnapped had changed him scared her.

"You have to tell me what you mean."

He looked as though he didn't want to speak.

"You're the one who brought it up!" she threw at him.

"Yeah. Because of the reason you came here." He shifted his weight from one foot to the other, then said, "Shelley, I've never told this to anyone. Well, I mean, my mom figured it out. But I never admitted anything—even to her. Especially to her."

She kept her gaze steady. "I'm still not following you."

"When I was kidnapped, I was just an ordinary kid. When I came back, I was different."

She wanted to scream at him. Whatever he was planning to say, he was dancing around it. "Spell it out,"

"Okay. I can make people do things."

"That's your terrible secret?" she shot back. "Well, what's the big deal? I can make people do things, too. I can make Trevor go to bed at bedtime. I can make his nursery school teacher be more sensitive to his needs." She bit her lip. "Well, I *could* do those things—before he disappeared. So what exactly do *you* mean?"

He thrust his hands into his pockets. "I mean that I can suggest a course of action—and the person will follow it. I don't mean I *say* or *do* anything. I just think about it—and they do it."

"That's…nonsense."

His stance turned aggressive. "Oh, yeah? So you think it was all your idea to leave me?"

"Of course it was!"

"Not true. I put the idea in your mind—and you did it."

"How?"

"I don't exactly know. I came back from those three missing months with the power to influence people."

She stared at him, trying to take that in, and trying to figure out what it meant to *him.* She'd driven here through a raging storm because she needed his help. Now it seemed as though he'd come unhinged. From the news that he had a son and that Trevor was missing? Or had it started earlier—when he'd walled himself off from the world?

As she regarded him, she started putting a bunch of things together, a bunch of things that added up to very odd behavior. He'd given up raising horses. He had an alarm system to warn him if someone was sneaking up on him. He was holed up here in this house like a hermit. He had a bunch of guns, not just normal rancher's hardware. And she was locked in here with him.

Suddenly, she was wondering what Matt Whitlock might do if he thought he was cornered.

When he started toward her, she cringed—giving away her fears.

He stopped short, staring at her. "You're afraid of me," he said in a flat voice.

"No."

He shook his head. "It's written all over your face, but I don't blame you."

"You say you have this talent—and you never told anyone about it," she challenged.

"That's right." He sighed.

"Why not?"

His expression turned glacial. "For starters, my mother tried to beat it out of me. I've told you what she was like. Strict. Absolutely certain of what was right and what was wrong. She used to talk about the neighbors. The people in town. She'd make judgments about them—and nobody ever came up to her standards. She even drove an extra fifty miles to a dry goods store because she didn't like Mr. Mason, the guy who owned the mercantile in Yuma." He took a breath.

"When she realized what I could do, she was sure it was the work of the devil. None of that made for an idyllic childhood."

Her heart squeezed, and she tried to imagine what it must have been like for him—if he was telling the truth.

He sighed. "I see you're having a little trouble with the concept. Do you want me to prove it?"

"How?"

"We'll call Ed Janey over from the bunkhouse, and I'll get him to do something."

"Maybe it will be something he was going to do anyway."

He laughed. "I mean, you can choose what you want him to do."

"Like what?"

"Anything."

She thought for a minute, trying to come up with something Matt wouldn't think of. Something that wasn't obvious. "You used to keep cans of vegetable beef soup in the pantry. Do you still?"

"Yes."

"Tell him to get a can from the shelf—and take it home," she tossed out, sure that would be the end of the experiment.

To her surprise, Matt said, "Okay. Come back to the kitchen and we'll call him."

He walked past her, and she could have refused to go along with this crazy plan. Instead she climbed off the couch and followed him down the hall.

When she stepped through the door, he was holding the receiver of the wall phone and dialing.

"Ed?" he said.

She couldn't hear the other end of the conversation, but she made sure Matt wasn't giving his foreman any clues.

"There's somebody over here who wants to say hello to you. Would you mind coming over?"

"Yeah. In this weather."

He hung up and turned to her. "He'll be here as soon as he can get his coat and boots on."

"Okay."

She walked to the table and picked up the mug of chocolate. It wasn't very hot anymore, but sipping it gave her something to do while she waited in the kitchen with a man who might be insane. She didn't want to think about it that way, but she couldn't stop herself from studying Matt's blue eyes, his mouth, his big rugged hands. He'd left his gun in the mudroom. Did he have another one in a kitchen drawer?

The clock on the wall ticked off the minutes, and she wondered if Ed was really coming. Or had Matt even spoken to Ed? Maybe this was all a sham. Like in a horror movie. She fought to get that notion out of her head.

When Matt saw her watching him, he went to the window and looked out at the wide expanse of white. A few minutes later, there was a knock at the back door. She heard someone stamping snow off his boots. Then Ed Janey came into the kitchen. He'd hung his coat up and was wearing jeans and a flannel shirt. His shoulders were a little stooped, his hair had gone completely gray, and his weathered face was more lined. But he had the same lean body that she remembered from when she'd lived at the ranch. They'd been friends back then.

"Shelley?" he said as soon as he saw her. "Is it really you?"

"Yes."

He crossed the kitchen and wrapped her in his arms. "It's so good to see you."

She swallowed around the lump in her throat. "And you, too."

"What brings you here?"

She glanced at Matt, then away. "I needed Matt's help with something," she said in a low voice.

Ed stepped back and studied her. "You got troubles, honey?"

"Nothing too bad," she managed to say.

He looked from her to the window and back again. "Heck of a day for a visit."

"I was passing by," she murmured, wondering if he believed her.

They chatted about old times for a few more minutes, and she heard regret in Ed's voice. Obviously he wished that Matt was working the ranch. Did the foreman feel useless? Probably, and that was a shame, because he'd been such an important part of the work life of the spread. Now he probably felt that he was living here on Matt's charity.

She wanted to ask him what he did all day now, but she understood that was a topic better left untouched.

When they came to the end of the conversation, he said, "Well, it's good seeing you, but I'd better be getting back."

As she watched him take a step toward the door, she wondered what kind of farce they'd been acting out. Did Matt really think he was going to get away with this insane tactic?

Maybe she'd be safer if she went back to the bunkhouse with Ed.

Chapter Three

Shelley's breath turned shallow as she watched Ed hesitate where he stood in the middle of the kitchen. For a moment, he looked totally confused. Then he made a little burbling sound in his throat and walked past her and into the pantry. When he emerged again, he was clutching a can of vegetable beef soup.

He stopped short, holding the can and looking at it as though it was a foreign object. "What am I doing?" he muttered. His expression changed to one of embarrassment as he glanced from the can to Matt. "This is yours. I should put this back."

"No. That's fine," Matt said. "I know you always liked it. Take it home and have it for dinner."

"You're sure?"

"Of course."

Still clutching the can, Ed hurried into the mudroom, and Shelley could hear his coat rustling.

Moments later, the back door slammed, and she was left alone with Matt who was gazing at her with what she could only call a smug expression on his face.

Her pulse was pounding as she looked back at him. She'd thought he was spinning a story—for some reason that she couldn't figure out. She'd thought maybe he was coming unglued. But he'd told her to pick something to have Ed do— and the man had done it. It had been entirely her choice.

Ed had hesitated at first, like he didn't know why he was getting the soup, but in the end, he'd followed what must have been Matt's silent directions.

All at once she was unsteady on her feet. Weak-kneed, she dropped into the nearest chair and grasped the edge of the table in front of her.

Matt stood across from her, his face turned to a mask of tension. "You still think I'm crazy?"

"I didn't say that."

"I don't have to be a mind reader to know what was dancing through your head."

She felt her cheeks flush. "I'm sorry. You've got to admit, it sounded…off the wall when you told me about it."

"Yeah. It takes some getting used to, all right. I sort of came to the realization gradually when I was a kid. At first I couldn't believe it myself."

"How did you discover something like that?"

He laughed. "I guess the first time was when I wanted to watch a TV program, and my mom wanted to make sure I'd done my homework first. It was a really important program. At least for a twelve-year old. A *Bonanza* rerun, I think. I silently asked her to let me watch instead, and she amazed me by doing it.

"Remember, I told you she was pretty strict. So her changing her mind was…unusual. The next time I tried it, I wanted chili for dinner. And I told her to make it—without saying anything out loud. She did."

"That must have given you a feeling of power."

"Yeah, but not for long. My mom was the kind of mother who watches for you to do something wrong so she can punish you."

Shelley winced, wondering what it would be like to grow up like that. Her own parents had always been warm and loving and supportive. They'd raised her to believe in herself and to take responsibility for her own decisions. They'd died before she knew she was going to have a baby, but their confidence in her had given her the courage to raise a child on her own. Sometimes it made her sad that Trevor would never know his grandparents. He'd never make cookies with her mom the way she had, or go fishing with her dad. And every holiday had had its traditions—like fun stocking stuffers at Christmas. She'd made sure to do all those things with her own son.

Matt was still speaking.

"Mom was smart. She caught on pretty fast—and started beating the crap out of me when she thought I was—she called it 'pushing' her. I guess that's as good a name as any for what I can do."

She nodded.

"And then she would go around talking to teachers and other people I knew, finding out if I'd 'pushed' them. So I had to be careful if I wanted to use it." He laughed. "Like once when I should have gotten detention, and I persuaded the teacher to let me off. Mom found out about it and made sure it never happened again."

Shelley's chest was so tight she could barely breathe. "I'm sorry. I had no idea about any of that."

"Of course not, because I never let on. It got stronger the older I got, but I used it less and less." He made a dismissive sound. "I think it's one of the reasons I'm good at training horses. I can get into their minds, too."

"That's fantastic."

"I decided it was weird."

Shelley was still taking everything in. Now that Matt was talking to her so openly, it seemed that she had missed so many opportunities to connect with him on a meaningful level when they'd been together.

"What did your mom think of your being kidnapped—and showing up again?" she asked.

"She never could explain it. And she acted like she thought I was lying about not remembering what had happened to me."

"She sounds…like a real gem."

He shrugged. "She died ten years ago." He grimaced. "I was sad, but I was relieved, too. Relieved to be free of the pressure of not antagonizing her."

Shelley winced. "When you were kidnapped, she told the authorities?"

"No. She thought I'd run away."

"A twelve-year-old?"

He shrugged again. "And she was determined not to have anyone think ill of her because of it. So she told folks I was visiting my uncle."

"That's child abuse."

He shrugged again.

"I don't dwell on my relationship with her." Switching back to the previous topic, he said, "I don't know how I got the talent. But I thought it had something to do with those missing months. I figured they'd done something to me. Something that—" he swallowed "—something that changed my DNA."

"Why would you think that?"

"Maybe because I read a lot of science fiction novels. Then, when I got older, I read scientific literature on the subject. Anyway, I didn't want to pass it on to any child of mine. That was why I vowed never to marry and never to have children."

Shelley looked out into the darkness, then back at Matt. "That's why you walled yourself off here?"

"Yeah. And…because I could never stop thinking that since I'd been taken away once, it could happen again. Now it has happened—but not to me."

"Oh, Matt."

He sounded so lost and defeated that she sprang out of the chair, crossed the distance between them and wrapped her arms around him.

As he stood rigidly in her embrace, she started speaking quickly. "It's not your fault. None of it is your fault. It's just something that happened to you."

"And to my son."

"But you came back."

"I was twelve. He's only…four."

When she pressed her face against his chest to muffle a sob, his arms came up to clasp her to him. "Shelley, I'm so sorry that I brought this on you—and Trevor."

"I'm sorry too," she whispered. "I should have told you about your son. I should have made you part of his life. He missed knowing my parents, and he missed knowing you."

"And you worked hard to make up for that."

"Yes. We could have had more money, if I'd taken more clients. But I spent time with him instead." She flapped her arm. "I felt guilty about that, too. I kept thinking that if I could have afforded a more expensive nursery school, he wouldn't have gotten stolen."

"Don't! They would have gotten to him some other way."

She went on as though he hadn't spoken. "I thought I was doing the right thing, but I know now that I was fooling myself. I was being selfish. I didn't want to get into a fight with you about my getting pregnant. So I just avoided the issue and kept Trevor all to myself."

He squeezed her tightly, then eased away. "Will you tell me about him?"

"Yes. I've got pictures in my wallet. Is my purse in the mudroom?"

"Yeah. Sorry. I should have given it to you."

"I didn't need it," she answered on the way to retrieve her purse. Opening her wallet, she got out a handful of pictures of a dark-haired little boy with blue eyes. The earliest one showed him in a high chair banging a plastic cup against the tray. Then there were two pictures of him at a playground. A school picture where he was posed against a blue background and a picture of him on a horse.

"He rides?"

"I figured he'd like horses. That was at a rodeo that came through Boulder."

"He looks like me," Matt marveled.

"Yes. I've got a lot more pictures at home. Not just pictures. I've got videos. And I try to write down the interesting or the funny things he does. I guess in the back of my mind I was keeping a record for you. But I couldn't admit that to myself."

"Tell me more about him."

"He's...sweet. And smart. He's memorized all the songs they sing at school. He loves to paint. He's already learning to read."

Matt looked impressed.

She laughed. "He likes chili. I guess he gets that from you. But it's hard to get him to drink his milk." She glanced at the mugs still sitting on the table. "I have to put chocolate in it."

Eagerly she went on to tell him so many of the things she hadn't been able to share with him. They made her feel closer to Matt—and to Trevor, too.

"It sounds like you're a good mother."

"I let somebody take him," she whispered, because she knew that if she tried to speak louder, she'd break down again.

"You couldn't guard him every minute. You had to work—to support him. Sending him to nursery school was a good option. And you had no idea that anyone was after him," he finished.

"Now it feels like I was living in a fool's paradise."

"I'm the one who would have been on guard."

"But you couldn't be. Because I didn't tell you."

He sighed deeply. "We'd better stop assigning blame. You came here so I could help you get him back. We'll do it."

She nodded, hope blooming inside her. She hadn't known

any of Matt's history, but knowing it made her feel as though they could find their son.

"You need to eat something. Then we'll get to work looking for him."

"Not the best conditions for traveling."

"We'll start with the computer. With abductions. The way the world is wired today, it's hard to keep anything in isolation—even when they told you not to talk about it."

"Okay."

He had just gotten up when a buzzer sounded, and she jumped.

"What's that?"

"The alarm. That's how I knew you were coming up the road."

Fear zinged through her. "You think somebody's watching the ranch? That they know I'm here?"

"I don't know, but better safe than sorry." He walked rapidly to the back entryway and took down a holster and a gun. Then he began getting into his cold-weather gear.

"What are you doing?"

"Going out to have a look. Like I did for you."

As she watched his preparations, she was thinking that in the normal course of events, he'd be considered paranoid for going out in the snow to make sure nobody was sneaking up on him. But it wasn't paranoia when you'd been kidnapped as a child, and when there had just been another kidnapping.

Still, she grabbed his arm before he could step out the door, and he turned to face her. "What?"

Her lips trembled. "If the kidnapper knows I'm here, they could hurt Trevor."

He stood looking at her, considering. "I think we have to assume that they want him for *something*, and they're not going to hurt him. They told you not to go to the authorities so they wouldn't have any interference."

"I guess that makes sense," she murmured.

"Just like they wanted me for *something*," he added.

"What?"

He swallowed. "To experiment on me, I guess."

Fear clutched at her insides again. "Do you think they'll do the same thing to Trevor that they did to you?"

"I don't know."

"I'm scared."

He nodded tightly.

"Are you thinking we should call the FBI?"

"Not yet. I'm thinking we should handle this by ourselves, under the radar—and use the FBI as a last resort. But I'd like to make sure we *are* under the radar."

"Yes," she agreed. She'd been on her own for so long, it was a relief to have someone else to share the decisions—and the worry. But she was going to carry her weight. Following him to the mudroom, she reached for her coat. "I'm coming with you."

"No. Stay here where it's safe."

"You could get Ed."

"I don't want to put him in danger—or anyone else."

Her heart started to pound as she peered into the darkness. "You think it's dangerous out there?"

"I don't know. But I've had a lot more experience with protecting myself than you have."

She wanted to ask what he meant—exactly. Had someone threatened him since the boyhood kidnapping? But she knew that this wasn't the time for questions, not when he needed to focus on whatever was out there. So she watched as he slipped out the door and into the frigid night.

Still, as he disappeared around the side of the house, she had to force herself not to follow him as another scenario zinged into her mind. What if they both had it wrong? What if someone was returning Trevor to them—at the ranch?

Her heart started pounding harder. Maybe that was it! Maybe all her fear and terror would be over soon.

Please, Lord, let that be true. Whoever had Trevor was returning him, just like they'd returned Matt. The same people? She didn't care at the moment. She just wanted to hold her son in her arms again and smother him with kisses. She wanted to make him laugh. And she wanted to run her fingers through his silky hair. So much. But she ordered herself not to clutch at straws. Why would someone kidnap Trevor—then bring him back?

It didn't make sense, but it was exactly what had happened to Matt. After three months, she reminded herself.

Feeling as if she'd caught the paranoia bug, she turned off the lights before walking to the window and staring out. When a shadow flitted by, she stiffened. Then she recognized Matt's tall form, checking out the ranch yard.

At least it was easy to do in this weather, she realized. If someone had come up to the house, he'd see tracks in the snow.

Her stomach clenched again as she remembered struggling up the road toward the house. But nobody would be foolish enough to leave a little boy out in the snow like that—would they?

She opened and closed her fists, forcing herself not to run outside. Trevor probably wasn't even here. Still, she couldn't stop herself from clinging to that hope because the thing she wanted most in the world was to get her little boy back.

Please, Lord, please. Let Matt come back with our son.

Every few moments, she glanced at the clock, keeping track of the time Matt had been gone. After five minutes, she started pacing the kitchen, returning to the window periodically to stare outside.

After ten minutes, she wanted to scream.

Why hadn't she insisted on going out there? It was all sh

could do to stay in the house—while she listened for the sound of gunshots.

But the only sound she heard was the pounding of blood in her ears. Until the back door opened, and Matt stepped back into the mudroom.

"Did you find Trevor?" she blurted as she turned the lights back on.

He tipped his head to the side, looking confused. "Trevor?"

She flushed, knowing that his mind hadn't taken the same leap as hers. "I…I was hoping that whoever took him returned him to us. Here."

Understanding bloomed on his face. "I'm sorry. I didn't find him."

"Okay," she answered, defeated.

He pulled off his coat and stamped snow off his boots.

"What did you find?"

"I think the only tracks leading up and down the road are yours and mine, although I can't be absolutely sure in the dark. Someone could have stepped in my footprints to disguise their trail."

"Okay."

"But I did see deer tracks down there. Maybe they set off the alarm."

She nodded. "I guess it was stupid of me to think someone would bring Trevor back—just like that."

"It could have been true—given what happened with me."

"But you don't remember anything from while you were gone."

"No!"

The way he said it made her throat tighten. "I'm sorry."

"If I remember anything, you'll be the first to know," he snapped, then looked apologetic. "Sorry, I'm on edge."

"We both are."

"There's a café in town that makes pretty decent chili."

"You're not suggesting that we go out, are you?"

Matt shook his head. "No. I bring it home in plastic containers. I thawed out a batch and stuck it in the refrigerator this morning." He laughed. "That sounds pathetic doesn't it?"

"Of course not. Cooking is a chore," she answered.

MATT COULD HAVE told her that he had plenty of time for chores. Instead, he opened the refrigerator and took out the carton.

"I'm not very hungry," she murmured.

"Neither am I. But we have to eat. We can each take a bowl of chili into the office while we do a computer search."

"Of what?"

"Missing children. I can't believe we're not going to find some cases that match Trevor's disappearance."

When he saw hope bloom on her face, he felt his chest tighten. So that she wouldn't see anything revealing in his eyes, he got out a glass bowl from a lower cabinet. After dumping the chili inside, he covered it with wax paper and set it in the microwave.

She'd come here because she had been at the end of her rope. Not like his mother who had pretended everything was fine and dandy while he was gone.

That told him something. She was a good mother to their son. And he was glad she had turned to him.

Could they find Trevor, then settle down together? His heart leaped at the thought. But was there any way to live as a normal family, or would there always be a threat hanging over him? Over them?

He struggled not to shudder, but she must have been watching him.

"What?"

"Nothing."

"Your shoulders are so rigid."

He made himself turn and face her. "This is a difficult situation, but we're going to get through it."

She gulped. "Are we going to find Trevor?"

"If it's humanly possible." He laughed. "And maybe my inhuman talent will help us."

"It's not inhuman."

"What would you call it."

"Extraordinary. Something that gives you an advantage over other people. In this case, over the bad guys—whoever they are."

He nodded. Although he hadn't thought of it that way, she was right.

Turning practical again, he asked, "What do you want to drink with dinner?"

She shrugged. "Coffee—if we're going to be up searching the Web."

He got a bag of coffee beans out of the freezer. While he ground the beans, she took down two bowls and spoons. They'd prepared a lot of meals together five years ago. It felt good getting back into that routine, but he reminded himself not to get too comfortable. She was only here to get his help in finding her son. Still, he couldn't stop himself from hoping for more.

They both carried their food and drinks to his study, where he cleared off a space on the desk. Then he pulled over the extra chair.

As he did, his hands tightened on the back. He'd bought the chair for her when she'd been doing his accounts, and the two of them had sat where they could both look at the computer screen.

They were going to do it again, but this time the mission was a lot more important than making sure the Silver Stallion Ranch wasn't spending more than it was taking in. They were going to find out what had happened to their son.

His son! He was still trying to wrap his head around that

concept, but the reality had taken hold as soon as she'd told him about Trevor.

He booted the computer, then took a spoonful of chili while he waited for the machine to go through its opening routine.

"I don't even know where to begin," she said as she watched his opening program bring up the news.

"Google," he said with confidence. He began by typing in a search field, then started cruising Web sites with information on missing children.

There was one site that listed children who had disappeared recently, but Trevor wasn't on it—because he had never been reported missing.

There was a site of "cold cases," but that, too, led to a dead end.

He checked law-enforcement sites in Colorado and surrounding states, then widened the search to the whole U.S.

When that didn't pan out, he went to private web pages of parents who were trying to find their children, but none of them seemed to have any relevance.

Beside him, he could feel Shelley willing him to find something—anything—that would help them.

A FEW HUNDRED FEET from the ranch road, in a patch of snow-covered pine trees, Bobby Savage and Don Campbell sat in a darkened sedan. Savage was blond with blue eyes. Campbell was dark.

Savage had a scar on his lip from an old knife fight. Campbell had a broken nose. He was a big guy with broad shoulders. Savage was smaller and quicker. But external appearances aside, they were very much alike. Either of them could kill a person as easily as they could run over a cat crossing the road.

They'd once enjoyed plenty of contract work in the New York/New Jersey area, doing whatever they were asked as long as the job paid well. Intimidation and murder were their specialties.

But after a job where they'd left some unfortunate evidence, the east coast had become a little hot for them. Since neither of them had enough money to retire comfortably, they'd accepted a gig out of Denver. After completing that assignment successfully, more jobs had rolled their way. The former city boys had adapted to working in the wide-open spaces of the west.

Too bad it was cold as a witch's lips out here.

"Turn up the heat again," Campbell said.

Savage reached for the control and cranked up the blower. As warm air flooded the car, Campbell sighed.

"This is a bitch of an assignment."

"The pay is good."

"But I don't like the way we're communicating with the guy who hired us."

"Advanced technology." Savage pulled out his BlackBerry and looked at the screen. There was nothing new. There had been nothing new for the past few hours.

"Does he think we're going to sit here all night?"

"I expect so."

Savage reached into the back seat and retrieved the bag of food they'd picked up at a fast-food restaurant in Yuma. Turning on a small flashlight, he directed the beam into the bag, then pulled out a wrapped hamburger that had gone cold hours ago. With a grimace he set it on his lap, then reached for the thermos of coffee that he'd stuffed into the door pocket.

"You're gonna have to get out and pee," Campbell cautioned, the idea of unzipping his fly in this weather making him shiver.

His partner gave him a knowing look. "Yeah. And eventually so will you—if we're gonna be here all night."

Savage craned his neck toward the ranch road. "I say they're not going anywhere until at least the morning."

"And your point is?"

"We could get a room in that town we passed and come back in the morning."

"You want to take a chance on losing them?"

Savage considered the question. He didn't know much about the man who had hired them, but he suspected that failure would be bad for their health.

With a sigh, he settled down in his seat for a long night in the cold.

BESIDE Matt, Shelley made a low sound. "This isn't doing any good."

He glanced over at her and saw that her hands were clasped tightly in her lap. It looked as though she was trying desperately to hold herself together, and he didn't blame her.

"Give me a little more time," he muttered.

"Okay."

Shelley leaned back and closed her eyes, and he knew she must be exhausted. She'd left Boulder early, then gotten caught in the storm, then come staggering up the road in snow up to her knees. He wanted to reach out and wrap her in his arms, but the rigid line of her jaw told him she didn't want comfort. She wanted results, although she didn't need to sit here while he tried to get them.

"Do you want to go to bed?"

Her eyes snapped open again. "No! I want to stay here in case you find something."

He didn't try to send her away again, because he knew that as long as he was sitting here, she was going to stay. She'd come to him for help, and he'd thought he could at least give them a start on the Web. He'd gone down a long list of sites, but he was losing faith in his ability to find anything. At least on this particular topic.

Still, he wasn't going to give up. Not while Shelley was sitting next to him, counting on him.

The Google entries were getting repetitive. He'd seen a lot of them before, but as he scrolled down, he spotted a new one that looked interesting. It wasn't from any organization. Instead it belonged to a man named Jack Maddox who was trying to find his missing brother, Jared.

Could this be the break he'd been looking for?

Matt clicked on the URL and waited with a sense of anticipation while the site loaded. Scrolling down, he saw something that made him gasp—a picture of an eight-pointed star.

Chapter Four

"What is it?" Shelley asked, her voice urgent.

Matt couldn't speak. As he stared at the image of the star on the screen, dark visions swam in his mind, memories that had never been accessible to him. Seeing that eight-pointed symbol had been like a mental door opening. Suddenly he knew where he had been when he'd been kidnapped all those years ago.

Beside him, Shelley turned in her seat and clamped slender fingers onto his arm. "Matt, what is it?"

With a hand he couldn't quite hold steady, he pointed to the strange-looking star.

"That."

"What is it?"

"I'm not sure. A symbol. As soon as I saw it, something leaped into my mind."

"Something like what?" she demanded.

The memory had been sharp and painful—and disturbing. If he told her, was she going to freak out like she had when he'd admitted his secret talent?

She wasn't giving him a choice. Tightening her hold on him, she demanded, "You have to tell me! You can't hold anything back because you think it's going to frighten me—or disturb me."

"I'm the one who's freaking out," he managed. "I told you that the time when I was kidnapped was a total blank. It was, but when I saw that star, I remembered...things."

"Bad things?" she asked in a strained voice.

"Yeah." He swallowed hard, wondering how he was going to say the next part. "A holding cell. There were bright lights over my head. They kept me awake. I'm sure there was a camera high up on the wall. I was alone. And scared."

She made a low sound. "That's when you were twelve?"

"Yes." Now that he'd told her that much, he found he needed to say the rest of it aloud—to make sure he wasn't making it up. "There was a narrow bed in the cell. Men would come in and take me down the hall to a...I don't know. It was like a doctor's office, I guess. They gave me all kinds of physical exams."

He gulped. "And they strapped me down and stuck needles into my back. Then into my arm."

She gasped. "Oh Lord. That must have been so awful. Do...do you think the same people have Trevor?"

"I don't know." *I hope not,* he silently added, knowing that she was probably thinking the same thing.

It was all he could do to stop himself from shaking. He wanted to be alone, to deal with this in private, but Shelley was sitting beside him, and he couldn't duck away from her. Not now.

"Why did they let you go?"

"I...I think I used my power to...give them a push. I mean, I put the suggestion into their minds, and they took me home."

"And you didn't have the power to do that—before they captured you?"

"Not hardly."

"So what they did to you—with those shots and all— caused it?"

"I think that must be true."

She ran a shaky hand through her hair as she took that in, then made a strangled exclamation.

"Will…Trevor…be able to do that?"

"I don't know!"

"If he could, they'd let him go."

"We hope."

She stared at him for a long moment, and he forced himself not to look away. Finally, she turned back to the computer screen.

"Don't you think that guy, Jack Maddox, was probably captured by the same people? I mean if he has that star on his Web site—and it made you remember what happened to you."

He nodded. The memories had excited him at first. Now they dug painful claws into the cells of his brain.

Shelley scrolled through the Web site. "Look. There's a phone number. We can call him and find out what he knows."

Matt felt desperation warring with hope. Maybe this man had some information that would lead them to Trevor, but he knew that they had to be cautious. "We can't call," he said.

Her instant disappointment tore at him. "Why not?"

"For starters, my phone might be tapped."

"Even your cell phone?"

"Yeah. And if they're listening in on me, they'll go right to Jack Maddox's house. Or—it could be a trap. Suppose it's not really a guy looking for his brother. Suppose the bad guys put up this site to find people they'd kidnapped when they were kids."

She winced. "Why would they do that?"

"Hell, I don't know. To get us back. Or to find out who remembers what. Maybe when somebody remembers they wipe out his memory again."

She gave a little nod. "I didn't think of that. It sounds so diabolical."

"Yeah, well, I've rolled it around in my mind for years."

"That's what you were doing when I'd wake up and find you lying there, and I'd know you hadn't been sleeping?"

"Yes."

"I wish I'd known what you were going through."

"I was hiding it from you—and everybody else. I wanted to seem normal."

"Oh, Matt."

"Don't pity me."

"I…" she stopped and started again. "You think someone is listening to your phone calls?"

"I don't know!" he answered, managing not to shout but knowing that he was going to lose control if he wasn't careful. He turned back to the screen. "Look at how this Web site is set up. Let's assume Maddox is for real. He's being cautious, too. He's not saying a lot. If I hadn't seen that star, I wouldn't have remembered anything. I wouldn't have thought about contacting the guy."

She scrolled through the material again and turned back to him. "I…guess you're right. We can't call, but what are we going to do?"

"Tomorrow, we go see the guy."

She looked from him to the screen and back again. "But he's in Rapid City, South Dakota."

Matt checked the mileage on Google. It's about 365 miles. We can be there in two hours."

She gave him a questioning look. "How?"

"We'll fly."

"But if we're trying to—" she stopped and gestured with her hand "—trying to hide our plans, won't there be a record of our reservations?"

"We're not making reservations. I have a Cessna at the Yuma Municipal Airport."

"A Colorado town of three thousand has an airport?"

"Yeah."

"Okay. And why do you have a plane there?"

He turned his hand palm up, thinking that they'd cut through a lot of his barriers in the short time she'd been here. He'd never discussed his feelings with anyone, but he was doing it now. "The ranch is my home. But sometimes I feel the place closing in on me, and I need to get away. When I do, I take off and fly somewhere I haven't been before—where I can lose myself for a while."

"It's because of that holding cell," she whispered.

"I guess so."

Because he was too restless to sit, he stood and walked to the window, where he stared out into the darkness, wishing he could blot out the scenes playing through his head.

He knew why he had wiped away the memories of his time in captivity. They were too awful for a twelve-year-old boy to remember and too awful for him now.

He heard Shelley push back her chair. Then he felt her hand on his shoulder.

"I'm sorry," she whispered.

He kept his back to her. "For what?"

"What you remembered. I can see it's…hurting you."

"Maybe that's my punishment for getting my son into this!"

"Lord, Matt. Don't ever say that. Your memories could help us find Trevor."

"I hope so."

"Would it be okay…if we talked about it a little more."

He forced himself to say, "Yes."

"So you were in a building?"

"I don't know. If it was, it didn't have any windows."

"What else could it have been?"

He sighed. "I guess it wasn't a boat."

"And you don't remember anything outside? You don't remember arriving?"

"I must have still been in that van, or I was out cold."

She made a low sound.

"All this speculation isn't doing either one of us any good."

"I see that." She stroked his arm, but he kept his body rigid. "Do you want me to leave you alone?" she asked in a small voice.

"That's the last thing I want." Turning, he reached for her, and she came into his arms. They clung together, each of them hurting, each of them needing comfort.

"Oh, Matt."

He stared down at her, meeting her eyes, and they moved at the same time. As he lowered his head, she raised hers, so that their mouths met. His reaction was swift and primal. He tightened his arms around her and kissed her hard, a desperate kiss filled with hunger, and he knew in that charged moment as his lips moved over hers that he needed her more than anything else in the world.

Was that okay? He couldn't decide, but he knew that they were both in a desperate situation. She was his only source of comfort, and he was hers. And he couldn't force his arms to turn her loose. Not unless she pushed him away or slipped out of his embrace.

When she stayed where she was, he angled his head one way and then the other, feasting on her, nibbling at her lower lip, sucking it into his mouth, taking the kiss to a level of instant intimacy that was only possible with lovers who knew each other well.

How could he have had the strength to send her away five years ago? He didn't know the answer. He only knew that having her in his arms again made his heart beat faster.

As he held her to him, his hands moved restlessly across her back, down her spine, to her hips, molding their bodies, sealing them with heat.

And to his shock and gratitude, she met his hunger with her own, her mouth exploring his, her hands clutching at him, pulling him closer. If a bomb had exploded outside in the darkness, he wouldn't have known it because the world had contracted to the woman in his arms. Her scent. The feel of her in his embrace. Her wonderful taste.

When she made a tiny, whimpering sound, it tingled along his nerve endings.

Lifting his head, he stared down at her. She looked dazed—as dazed as he felt.

He wanted her, and every masculine instinct urged him to rush her into the bedroom before she changed her mind, but he couldn't do that. He had to give her a chance to decide what was right for her.

"Will you come to my room?" he asked in a thick voice, then waited with his heart pounding.

"Yes."

"You're sure?"

"Yes."

He celebrated the answer with another kiss. Greedy for more, he swept his tongue into the warmth of her mouth, investigated the inside of her lips, the serrated edges of her teeth, the sensitive tissue beyond.

In response, she moaned into his mouth, her tongue no less bold as it found his, then stroked the insides of his lips.

Need made him press her body more tightly to his as his hands swept up and down her back, cupped her bottom, lifted her against his erection.

When they finally came up for air, he took her hand and led her down the hall, past the room where she had slept earlier and into his bedroom—the room they had once shared.

He had thought she would never come to the Silver Stallion Ranch again. Now she was back. He would have called it a miracle, only the reason was all wrong.

Tomorrow, they would have to deal with that. Tonight, they both needed comfort and consolation.

Stepping away from her, he turned on the bathroom light, then closed the door most of the way so that there was enough illumination to see her but not too much to break the spell.

Desperate to feel her satin skin against his, he yanked his shirt over his head and tossed it away. When he looked up, she had pulled off her blouse and was reaching around to unhook her bra.

She seemed to be caught in the same wild surge of need as he. Pulling off her borrowed sweatpants, she kicked them away, along with her panties.

Reaching for him, she began undoing his belt buckle while he unsnapped his jeans and lowered the zipper.

They both tugged at his pants, dragging them down, so that he was naked in seconds and pulling her into his embrace.

A strangled cry rose from his throat, or perhaps from hers as he clasped her in his arms, pressing her naked body tightly to his, then easing away just a fraction so that he could sweep her wonderful breasts back and forth across his chest.

They were fuller now. A woman's breasts, and he thought she must have nursed their child. But he didn't ask because he didn't want the pain of loss to intrude on this moment. He wanted only the two of them in this room, giving to each other and receiving.

"Oh!" she cried out as the twin points of her nipples dragged across the hair of his chest.

He remembered this, remembered all of it. Yet he marveled at the intensity of what he felt now.

Closing his eyes, he trailed his hands down her back, over her rounded bottom, touching her everywhere he could reach.

They moved together toward the bed, and he bent to pull the covers back so that they could both slip under.

Rolling to his side, he lowered his head to take one of her distended nipples into his mouth, drawing on her as her hands came up to clasp the back of his head and hold him to her.

"Matt. Oh, Matt, I told myself I didn't need you. I was lying to myself."

"So was I."

Reaching between them, she found his taut, aching flesh, closed her hand around him, stroked him the way she knew he liked.

He had never needed a woman more than he needed Shelley. Now. And at the same time, her pleasure had become the center of his universe.

She was offering him a precious gift, and he wasn't going to accept it without knowing she was with him every step of the way.

He touched her and kissed her, tasted her, lifting his head to watch her face and judge her readiness as he stroked his fingers through her most intimate flesh. The passion smoldering in her eyes told him what he needed to know.

"Matt…now…please." She rolled to her back and reached for him again, her hand firm on his erection as she guided him to her.

His body sank into hers, and he felt as though he had come home after a long, lonely trip through a wasteland that he couldn't even describe.

Lifting his head, he stared down at her.

"I was a fool to give you up," he whispered as he began to move inside her.

She matched his rhythm, clung to his shoulders, climbed toward orgasm with him. The tension was almost unbearable as he held himself back, waiting for her to reach the peak of her pleasure. When he felt her start to contract around him, he let go, climax rocking his body and rocking his soul. Their lovemaking had been intense before, but never like this because now they shared a sorrow neither of them could express in words.

As the storm passed, she moved her lips against his

cheek, clasped him tightly when he tried to shift his weight away from her.

"Stay."

He gathered her to him, rolling to his side, still inside her, holding her as he finally let himself drift off to sleep.

AND IN THE MORNING, when he woke up at seven, she was gone from the bed—as he knew she would be.

Quickly he climbed from under the covers, then strode to the bathroom where he used the facilities, showered and shaved. He could have gone looking for her right away. But he was postponing the discussion they were going to have.

Finally, when he was dressed and feeling a little more in control, he followed the smell of fresh coffee down the hall to the kitchen. She had also dressed in jeans and a flannel shirt, clothing of hers that she had left here five years ago. And she'd found it in the storage closet.

Her back was to him, and she seemed to be staring out the window.

"Look at me."

When she turned to him, her eyes were red-rimmed.

"Don't tell me we did anything wrong last night," he said in a gritty voice. "We needed each other. You know that as well as I do."

"And our little boy could be in a holding cell with bright lights keeping him awake!"

"Don't."

"I'm just trying to…"

"Make us both feel guilty," he supplied.

She raised her chin. "Shouldn't we feel guilty?"

He kept his gaze on her. "Think about it this way. Five years ago, I sent you away because I thought it was the right thing to do. If I hadn't, I would have had the happiness of the two of you with me. I denied myself that. Now I've got the pain of losing my son—without ever having met him. And the pain of knowing that I put him in danger."

Before he finished speaking, she made a little gasping sound. "Oh, Matt. I wasn't thinking of all that. I was just feeling terrible because I let myself take comfort from you because I needed you so much. Then in the morning I felt…like I'd betrayed Trevor."

Quickly she crossed the distance between them and pulled him close. His arms came up to embrace her, and they stood in the middle of the floor, holding each other.

They clung together for long moments, swaying slightly. When he finally eased away, he saw tears in her eyes. One spilled out and trailed down her cheek. Raising his hand, he wiped it away with his knuckle.

"We'll find him," he said.

"Yes."

He might have added, *I can't promise I'll keep my hands off you while we're together.* But he left that and a lot of other things unsaid.

"I remember you like a good breakfast," she said briskly. "Do you want eggs and bacon?"

"Yeah. Thanks."

They both ate quickly. Then he went back to the computer to plot a route to Rapid City, South Dakota.

Next he walked over to the bunkhouse to tell Ed Janey that they would be away for a few days and that he wouldn't be able to call. Finally, he tramped down the road a ways, looking at the boot tracks. Unfortunately, it seemed that Ed had also gone down the road to have a look at Shelley's car, obscuring any tracks from the previous night.

After getting Shelley's bag out of the car, he evaluated the condition of the access road. The snow wasn't too deep, and he figured that the four-wheel drive would make it to the highway.

"Do you mind leaving your car where it is?" he asked Shelley.

"No. Because I don't want to take the time to dig it out."

They were in his Cherokee and on the ranch road just after eight.

Almost as soon as he turned onto the highway, he saw a dark SUV pull out of a side lane and fall into place behind them.

When he speeded up, the other car did, too. When he slowed down, the other guy kept pace.

"Damn," he muttered.

Shelley turned toward him in alarm. "What?"

"Somebody's following us."

"What are we going to do?"

"Lose them, I hope. Can you see who they are?"

TREVOR ROLLED into a ball and closed his eyes. The man named Blue had stuck another needle in him. In his arm, not his back this time. Now his head hurt, and when he opened his eyes, everything looked funny.

"Mommy," he whispered. "Please come get me, Mommy. I don't want to stay here."

She didn't answer because she was somewhere far away. And he was afraid he was never going to see her again.

As he thought of that, his throat got tight, and he squeezed his eyes shut. When he was sure he wasn't going to cry, he opened his eyes again and yanked at the chain that held him to the bed. If only he could slip his hand out of the cuff, he could run away.

He didn't know where he was, but Mommy had told him what to do if he got lost. He was supposed to find a policeman, and they'd take him back to Mommy.

He said his name and his address and phone number. He was a big boy, and he knew all that stuff. He could tell them exactly who he was, and they'd take him home. If he could just get away from Blue.

"Mommy," he whispered again, knowing it was silly to think that she could hear him. Yet he couldn't stop himself from believing that it might be true.

SHELLEY TWISTED AROUND, looking through the back window at the car following them. "The glass is tinted. I can't see who's inside."

"Of course."

He kept driving down the road for several miles, until they reached a part of the highway where rock outcroppings had forced the engineers to work around several sharp turns. As soon as he was well into the rocks, he turned to Shelley. "Hold on."

She grabbed the handle above the door as he speeded up, rounding a curve and pulling off the blacktop onto a side road where a towering rock blocked the view of his vehicle.

The other car sped past, and he waited long enough to make sure that the driver thought he was still heading west.

When he pulled out, he turned east, hoping that the other car would continue on for a few more miles before the driver figured out he was going the wrong way.

BOBBY SAVAGE sped down the blacktop, trying to catch up with the man who had just executed a bunch of tricky moves on his home turf. That was the problem with working out here in the middle of nowhere. The natives knew the territory, and he didn't.

The farther he got from the ranch, the more convinced he was that somehow Matt Whitlock had given them the slip.

Finally, he pulled to the side of the road.

"What are we gonna do?" Campbell asked.

"Call for instructions. I got a hint from the boss that there's a way to find these two."

"Then why were we sitting outside the ranch house all night?"

"Don't ask me. Maybe he doesn't have the other thing set up yet. Or maybe he wanted to find out how good we are."

"And we just showed him we lost the son of a bitch," Campbell muttered.

Savage turned to his associate. "You want to keep driving? Like to California, and start again? I hear there's contract work in San Francisco."

His partner shook his head. "I get the feeling that this guy we're working for would find us."

Savage sighed. "Agreed."

"So make the call."

He pulled out his BlackBerry and pressed a speed-dial button, waiting with his heart pounding for the expression of disgust on the other end of the line.

"IT'S GOING to take longer to get out of town," Matt told Shelley as he made a left turn onto a secondary road that looked as though it had been plowed halfway through the storm. He struggled to keep up some speed under the hazardous conditions.

"That's better than having someone know where we're going."

As he circled back toward the airport, he saw Shelley sitting with her knuckle between her teeth.

"What?" he asked gently.

"If they know we're looking for Trevor, they could hurt him."

"I don't think they will," he said again. Maybe if he kept repeating it, it would turn out to be true.

"But you don't *know!*"

He reached for her hand. "Do you want to call the FBI?"

"No!"

"I think our best bet is to talk to Jack Maddox, then decide on our next move."

She nodded.

The roundabout route and the poor driving conditions added an extra hour to the morning's drive.

When they finally arrived at the airport, Matt filed a flight plan and checked out his plane. He'd never given false information before, but he didn't want anyone to know his destination. So he said he was heading for Oklahoma City.

"You didn't fly when I knew you," Shelley said as she eyed the single-engine plane.

"After you left, I took flying lessons to give myself something to do."

"Okay."

"You look nervous."

"I've never flown in a small plane before."

"Relax. I'm a good pilot."

"How do you know how to get from here to Rapid City?"

"Well, I know the direction. It's almost straight north. I've got a GPS, and I'll look for landmarks on the ground. Like highways and rivers and Mount Rushmore. That will be a big clue that we've arrived."

She eyed his plane, then let him lead her to the door and help her inside.

After checking everything, he got clearance from the airport and headed for the runway.

As he took off, he gave her a sideways glance and saw her hanging on to the edge of her seat, staring straight ahead. But once they were in the air, she relaxed and looked out the window.

"So what do you think?" he asked.

"It's not so different from flying in a bigger plane."

"Yeah, but there's not as much stability if we hit rough air."

"Now you tell me."

Despite the warning, there were no rough patches.

Two hours after they'd taken off, they landed at the Rapid City

Regional Airport. Because Matt hadn't called ahead, he was worried about picking up a rental car. But he found a rental office at the airport, and they headed toward the outskirts of the city.

"What if Jack Maddox isn't home?" Shelley asked.

"Let's not worry about that until it happens."

"Or what if he's not who he said he is?"

"I guess we have to take a chance on that."

She sighed. "I'm nervous. Scared he can't tell us anything and scared that he can."

"Yeah."

The address was outside of town, in a wooded area. They found the street number and turned in at a long driveway flanked by tall pines. The house was a one-story cabin nestled in the woods with a gabled entrance and a porch that ran the length of the front.

There were no lights on inside, and as they approached the house, Matt saw no cars, which didn't mean anything, since there was a detached garage.

They climbed out, and Matt stood for a moment, getting the lay of the land. He could hear the sound of a nearby creek flowing over rocks. As they walked toward the door, Matt thought he saw a window curtain move, but maybe it was only his imagination.

When he knocked, nothing happened.

"I guess he's not home."

"Maybe."

They waited for several more seconds, and Matt was about to walk around the back of the house when he heard a voice from behind them say "Hands in the air. Turn around slowly. No tricky moves—or you're dead."

Chapter Five

Matt heard Shelley gasp.

"It's okay," he said, hoping it was true.

They both raised their hands and turned to confront a tall broad-shouldered man with short-cropped black hair and blue eyes. He was holding a gun pointed at them, and Matt wished he'd brought his Glock with him, although maybe that was a recipe for disaster. The guy was already on edge.

"Jack Maddox?"

"Who wants to know?"

"My name is Matt Whitlock. This is Shelley Young. Our son has been kidnapped."

The big man made a snorting sound. "Yeah, you used that kidnapped kid trick on me before. At Mount Rushmore."

Huh? What was this guy talking about? Trying to get his message through, Matt plowed ahead. "It's no trick. We were searching the Web for sites on missing children and saw your page—with your plea for information about your brother. That's why we're here."

"Why didn't you call—instead of just showing up?"

"Because I think my phone is tapped," Matt answered, working hard to keep his voice even. "We were followed from my ranch outside Yuma, Colorado, by guys in a black car."

Maddox's face hardened. "That's just great. So you led them here?"

"No. We gave them the slip and left in my plane from the Yuma airport."

Shelley broke into the conversation, her voice high and strained. "Please, Mr. Maddox, my little boy is missing. He's only four. I know he's frightened."

Maddox answered with a hard stare, as if he thought she was making up a story.

Shelley gave him a pleading look. "Our son *is* missing. And the same thing happened to Matt when he was twelve. Last night when he saw that eight-pointed star on your Web site, he remembered being captured and held in a cell. He remembered men sticking needles in his back and his arm."

Maddox made a moaning sound as though a painful memory had just grabbed him by the throat.

"Did that happen to you?" Shelley pressed.

Instead of answering, Maddox zeroed in on Matt, his voice edged with steel. "If you're telling the truth—what's your talent?"

Matt blinked. "What?"

"What's your talent? What paranormal ability did you acquire from those injections they gave you?"

Matt shook his head, trying to make sense of the conversation. "How do you know about that?"

"Because that's their purpose—to give you some special ability that humans don't ordinarily have."

Matt had thought something like that himself. But it had all been about him—not anybody else.

"There are different ones?"

"Yeah."

Seeing the intensity on the other man's face, he figured he'd better answer the question. "Okay. I can influence other people's behavior." He shook his head. "I guess I should have been working on you—getting you to put away that gun, but I didn't think of it."

The man snorted. "Well, it sounds like you're legit, because nobody would make up that answer. Sorry for the gun. I tend to be a little paranoid." He shoved the weapon into the waistband of his pants. "You can put your hands down."

"Thanks." They both lowered their hands, and Matt saw his relief mirrored on Shelley's face.

"I've been on edge all day—knowing somebody was going to show up here. But I didn't know who or why. That's *my* talent. Precognition. Seeing the future. But it's not always crystal-clear."

As Matt absorbed that news, he reached for Shelley's gloved hand, squeezing it tightly. "Okay?" he asked.

She gave a little nod.

"Come on in."

Maddox rapped on the door—two short and one long knock. A woman with curly blond shoulder-length hair opened the door.

"I heard all that," she said. "I'm Claudia Reynolds." She looked around. "Let's not stand out here."

They all walked into the house, which was small and homey—like the exterior.

The man with the gun turned to them. "I never did introduce myself. I'm Jack Maddox. But I guess you already figured that out."

"Matt Whitlock and Shelley Young," Matt repeated.

"Let me take your coats. Come sit down. Can I get you something?"

"No thank you," Matt answered.

They took off their outerwear, which Maddox hung on a rack in the hall before leading them into a living room furnished with a large leather love seat and sofa. Matt and Shelley took the love seat.

"I'm sorry to barge in on you like this," Shelley said.

"No problem," Jack answered.

"All we want is our son," Shelley continued.

Claudia gave her a sympathetic look. "We'll tell you what we can."

"Thank you."

Jack and Claudia took the couch. Their host studied Matt. "How long did they have you?"

"Three months. I think I used my talent to convince them to let me go."

"Three months." Jack whistled through his teeth and glanced at Claudia. As Matt saw their eyes meet, he was thinking that maybe the man had been missing for a week or something.

Jack's next words came like a shower of freezing water. "They had me and my brother for fifteen years."

Shelley gasped and clamped her hands to her mouth. "Oh Lord, that's horrible."

Jack shrugged. "I didn't have much choice about it."

"But he eventually escaped," Claudia said. "I found him wandering around in the woods. In a rainstorm. I took him home and tried to figure out who he was, but he didn't remember anything."

"Neither did I," Matt agreed. "The missing months were an absolute blank. Until I saw that star on your Web site. Then some nasty memories came zinging back to me. I guess it's a symbol—but maybe it's also a kind of subliminal message."

"Yeah."

Matt and Jack stared across the space that separated them, sharing an experience that few people could imagine. Or would *want* to imagine. For years Matt had felt alone, now here was a man who had gone through the same thing—only a thousand times worse. They'd had him for years, not months.

Jack reached for Claudia's hand, and Matt watched silent

communication pass between them. The big man shifted in his seat. "So my Web site got a response, but you're not saying you can help find my brother."

"I'm sorry," Shelley whispered. "When Matt saw the eight-pointed star, it triggered buried memories. But it was only about him—not you or your brother. We're here because we're desperate to find Trevor. He's only four. He's got to be scared out of his mind."

Claudia nodded. "I understand."

"If you're worried about them coming after you again, why did you put your address on the Web site?"

"Like I said, I have an early warning system. And I was desperate to find Jared."

"It's the same for us. We're desperate, and we'd be grateful for any information you can give us," Shelley continued. "Anything." She stopped and cleared her throat. "Something else I didn't tell you. Whoever took Trevor warned us not to contact the FBI or the police—or they'd hurt our son. So we haven't done that."

Again Claudia gave her a sympathetic look. "I'm sorry, but most of what we learned is from the FBI. We talked to them after—we escaped."

Shelley's hand tightened on Matt's.

"So if you absolutely don't want the FBI involved, you'd better get up and leave," Claudia continued.

Matt turned to Shelley. "We already decided that warning was a lie—to keep the authorities out of the picture, right?"

Her lips trembled. "I hope so." Turning back to Claudia, she said, "Please give us some information that would help us find our son. Anything!"

The way she said *our* made Matt's heart squeeze. He'd only found out yesterday that he had a child. Shelley had brought him into the picture because she needed his help. Would she keep him in the picture once they found Trevor?

He couldn't even be sure it was the right thing for the three of them. He already knew he was a threat to their safety, but he vowed they were going to find Trevor. He couldn't entertain the idea of failure.

Jack Maddox stood up and paced to the window, where he lifted the curtain and looked out. Probably he'd gotten into the habit of checking the area—even if he did have some knowledge of the future.

When he stiffened, Matt stood too. "What?"

"I don't know…"

He strode back to the hall and grabbed his coat. When Matt also went to get his coat, Jack shook his head. "Stay here."

"Let me go with you."

"It's better if only one person is a target."

He walked to the back of the house and slipped out the door, gun in hand.

Shelley and Claudia had also stood, and the three of them moved to different windows, each of them easing the shade aside so they could peek out. Nobody remarked that Jack was paranoid. They were all willing to believe the house might be surrounded—which was a horrifying conclusion.

Matt felt his heart beating as long minutes passed. Finally footsteps sounded on the back porch, and he whirled to face whoever was coming through the door.

It was Jack. "I don't see any tracks."

"Good," Claudia said in a matter-of-fact voice, and Matt had the impression that they enacted similar scenes on a regular basis.

Jack took off his coat and rolled his shoulders. "Sorry. I thought I heard something." He looked at Claudia and then away. "I get…nervous."

"So do I," Matt answered. "I don't have your sixth sense for the future, so I have an alarm system."

"Byproduct of captivity," Jack muttered as he sat down

again. The three of them followed him to the seating area. "Maybe I'll get over it sometime."

"Yeah," Matt answered, wondering if he'd ever feel safe in his own home. He'd been cautious for years. Now he knew he hadn't been overreacting.

When they were settled again, Jack looked at Matt. "I'm pretty sure both you and I were held at a place they call the Facility. It's under a mountain and goes back to Cold War days. Probably it started out as a fallout shelter. Then it got turned into a secret laboratory."

Matt nodded. "So that's why there were no windows."

"Yeah," Maddox agreed.

"Who was running the lab?" Matt asked.

Claudia shifted in her seat. "I was part of it. Well, not at that exact location."

Matt's attention jerked toward her. "Did I hear that right?"

Jack slipped his arm around Claudia. "She didn't know what she was really involved in. She was a researcher working for a Dr. Thomas Lasher, an expert in physics, psychology and artificial intelligence—on a project to interface people with precognition and machines."

BOBBY SAVAGE, pressed the off button on the phone and looked at Campbell. "The most likely scenario is that they've flown to Rapid City, South Dakota."

"You're kidding, right?"

Bobby sighed. "I wish I were. Our instructions are to fly there, then wait for a special delivery package."

"What kind of package?"

"The instructions will be included."

Campbell's eyes narrowed. "I don't like it. I mean, what if they're not there?"

"Then it won't be our fault. Come on, we've got to hustle to make the next flight."

CLAUDIA BEGAN to speak again. "Dr. Lasher told me his dream was to create a fusion of man and machine that would be able to detect and maybe prevent global catastrophes."

Too edgy to keep his tone even, Matt snapped, "That sounds like a plot for a science-fiction novel."

"Everything that's happened to you and me sounds like a science fiction plot, don't you think?" Jack asked.

"You have a point."

"That's not the half of it," Claudia continued. "Dr. Lasher was working with a Dr. Kenneth Sykes, whose initial goal in the Vietnam era was to create super soldiers using gene manipulation. That experiment was a bust. But Sykes was able to build on his research. He discovered the techniques he'd developed worked best in people who carried a certain recessive gene, which he called *I,* for Ideal. He'd give them a certain combination of drugs that activated the recessive genes, which in turn gave them heightened abilities."

Matt leaned forward. "Are you saying this is a government conspiracy?"

"I guess it started out as a government project. But then somebody got cold feet. Or maybe the results didn't justify the expenses. At any rate, Sykes went off on his own."

Matt nodded. "So I guess you and I have that recessive gene?"

"Yeah. And unfortunately for us, Sykes also discovered that the younger the individual was when the treatment began, the more developed their abilities would become. So he started looking for kids to test. That's how my brother and I ended up in the program. And you."

Matt fought a wave of sickness. When he'd started looking for Trevor, he hadn't considered that diabolical scientists were using innocent Americans like lab rats. But that's exactly what Jack was telling him. He'd been part of the monstrous experiment. Now his son was in the middle of it, and that was Matt Whitlock's damn fault—no matter what anyone tried to tell him.

Claudia was speaking again in a halting voice, and he brought his mind back to her words. "I was working with a test subject. Someone I hadn't met, and they wouldn't tell me who it was. All I knew was that it was someone who could influence a Random Event Generator on the computer. Long story short, it turned out to be Jack. And he was trying to warn me that I was in danger. Then Dr. Lasher was murdered, and I decided to pull a disappearing act. Something made me come to this area. I rented this cabin and supported myself as a Web designer."

Jack picked up the story. "My brother and I escaped from the Facility, but we knew our best chance to stay free was to separate. I was pretty out of it, but something drew me here— looking for Claudia, even when I hadn't met her and I didn't exactly remember who she was."

"How could you find her, if you didn't know her?"

"When we were doing those Random Event Generator experiments, I forged a mental connection with her." He laughed. "There are some advantages to developing special powers."

"How is this going to help us find Trevor?" Shelley asked. "Do you think he's being held at that place—the Facility?"

"No," Jack said immediately. "The FBI shut it down after they found out that Sykes was using the place."

"You know where it is?"

"Yeah. I can give you a number to call—if you want to follow that lead," Jack said.

"Appreciate it," Matt answered.

After talking to Jack and Claudia, they had a lot more background information, but Matt wasn't sure that got him and Shelley any closer to Trevor. In fact, he was beginning to think that he should send Shelley back to the ranch while he continued hunting for their son. But he wasn't going to bring that up until they were alone. Maybe he wasn't going to bring it up at all. He'd just use his power on her and get her out of danger.

"I guess this is a lot bigger than we realized," he said.

"Exactly."

"We have a ton of thinking to do. Probably we should find a motel in the area."

"You could stay here with us," Claudia offered.

Matt shook his head. "That's kind of you, but from what you've been saying, it's probably safer if we separate."

Jack agreed. "Let us know when you find your son," he said, as though it was a foregone conclusion.

Matt's throat tightened, but he managed to say good-bye and shake hands with the guy.

Shelley and Claudia embraced. "If there's *anything* we can help with, please let us know," she said.

They left and drove back toward Rapid City, with Matt checking frequently in the rearview mirror to make sure nobody was following them. As far as he could tell, they were in the clear.

When he cut Shelley a sideways glance, she turned to him. "I know you're blaming yourself."

"You don't think I should?"

She waited several beats before saying, "You've been carrying this around for a long time, but there's something you may not have caught." The way she said the last part made his hands tighten on the wheel.

"What?"

"Jack said the I trait is caused by a recessive gene."

"And your point is?"

"You can't inherit a recessive gene from just your mother r your father. You have to get a copy from each parent. Take ars for example."

"What about them?"

"Most people have free-hanging earlobes." She pulled gently on the bottom of his ear. "We both do. That's from the dominant gene. But some people have attached ear lobes, which comes from a recessive gene. If you have them, you got them from both your mother and your father. Of course, that doesn't mean both parents have attached earlobes. It just means they have the recessive gene."

"How do you know all that—about genes?"

"I took biology in college. The important point is that you have to get a recessive gene from both parents to have the trait. That means Trevor had to get it from *both* of us. Not just from you."

He realized with a jolt that she was right. He'd been blaming himself, and he hadn't caught that little detail.

"It's my fault, as much as yours," she murmured, in case he was still missing her point. "The only difference is that we know that giving you their voodoo injections triggered a paranormal power. We don't know if it would work on me."

"Because nobody kidnapped you! Thank God."

"I guess they could have. And they've obviously been keeping track of me and Trevor. They must have done genetic testing on him—without my knowledge."

Matt couldn't hold back a string of profanity. "Those bastards! Who the hell do they think they are?"

"I guess they think that their nasty little science experiments are more important than our rights as American citizens," she said.

He had been thinking something very similar.

"At least we're not flying blind anymore," she said. "The more we know, the more chance we have of finding Trevor."

He hoped that was true. He didn't point out that they already knew of at least one murder associated with the project. How many more didn't they know about?

Another terrible thought struck him, and he struggled not

to let anything show on his face. But he was suddenly wondering how many children had been kidnapped and what had happened to them. How many of them hadn't survived the treatment they'd been given to turn on the I gene?

He'd never had much faith in prayer. Probably because of his mother's brand of religion. But now he was hoping God would see fit to help a little boy in trouble.

Please, Lord. Let Trevor make it through this. Please, Lord. I haven't asked you for much. But I'm asking for my son. And for Shelley.

He made the request over and over—until Shelley cleared her throat.

Feeling as if he'd been caught doing something he shouldn't, he glanced at her, half expecting her to make a comment. Instead, she had a look on her face that told him she was feeling unsure of herself, too.

"What is it?" he asked.

"Can you tell me when they started giving you injections?" she asked in a voice that was barely above a whisper. "I mean, was it right away? Or did they wait?"

He thought for a moment, but he couldn't come up with an answer. The time he'd been in captivity had just been one long period of terror for a twelve-year-old boy. "I'm sorry. I don't remember that kind of detail."

"Maybe they don't do it right away," she said, her voice still very low. "You said they tested you first."

"Yeah," he agreed, not because he believed it in this case. He'd been in a secure facility. Trevor was God knew where.

"Do you remember anything else specific?"

"Like what?"

"Did they give you decent food?"

"I think so."

"And nobody…hurt you. Except for those injections they gave you."

"I think that's right," he answered, knowing that she was trying to assure herself that her son wasn't being mistreated—apart from the basic fact that they were doing diabolical experiments on him without even pretending to ask permission.

As they drew closer to town, they must have silently agreed to stop torturing themselves with speculation about Trevor, because they dropped the conversation and started looking for a place to stay.

Since Rapid City was smack in the middle of a scenic area, with everything from the famous giant presidents' faces on Mount Rushmore to horseback-riding, ice-fishing and rock-hounding, there was no shortage of motels in town. Some were closed for the winter, but lots of them were open—ranging from luxury resorts to more basic accommodations.

Matt found a small motel, the Stone Monument, that was well off Highway 90. It wasn't anything fancy, but it was in a wooded area with the rooms in separate cabins, which would give them some privacy.

He checked them in, signing the guest card with the fake name and I.D. he'd gotten a few years ago in case he needed it. He also gave them a fake license plate number and paid in cash.

As soon as he'd shut the door behind them, he felt the room closing in on him and knew it was a reaction to the intensity of the conversation with Jack and Claudia. It was simply too horrifying to absorb in only a few hours.

"Don't," Shelley whispered.

"Don't what?"

"Try to take all the blame. I told you, it's as much my fault as yours."

When he didn't answer, she reached for him and pulled him into her arms. And once she did, he couldn't stop himself from clasping her to him and holding on tightly.

He wanted to tell her everything was all right, but he

couldn't get the words past his parched lips, so he just stroked his hands up and down her back and across her shoulders, taking comfort from the contact.

Wishing he could shut away the world, he closed his eyes, swaying slightly as he held her. They'd made love last night. Lord, was it only last night? So much had happened that it seemed like a month ago.

Her head dropped to his shoulder, and he felt her tremble. He wasn't the only one suffering from the shock of what they'd heard from Jack and Claudia. This whole damn mess was too much for her. Too much for anyone to bear, come to that, and he wanted to know she was out of danger.

He understood she wasn't going to back away voluntarily, but Jack had pointed out that there were advantages to having special powers, and he was going to cash in on his abilities now. With his eyes still closed, he started sending her a silent message, using the talent that Dr. Sykes and his researchers had given him.

Shelley, you want to go back to the ranch. You want to go to the ranch where it's safe. You want to wait for me there while I look for Trevor. You want to be at the ranch. We can call Ed Janey and tell him you're coming.

As he held her and stroked her, he kept repeating the message over and over, confident that it must be getting through to her—until her arms came up, and she pressed against his chest, pushing him away. Hard.

"Matt Whitlock, what do you think you're doing?" she demanded.

"Nothing."

"Don't tell me 'nothing.' You're trying to use that damn power of yours to send me back to Colorado."

He stared at her. "What makes you think so?"

Her eyes were fierce.

"Because I just got an overwhelming urge to go back to the ranch."

"It's a good idea."

"I don't think so. In fact, there is no way on God's green earth that I would have thought of it myself. Which means you put it in my mind."

The challenging look on her face made his insides knot, but he stood his ground, because he knew he had been doing the right thing, even if she didn't agree.

"Okay! We're back in business," Bobby Savage crowed as he brought the air express package to the rental car.

Don Campbell watched while his partner took a penknife to the wrapping and carefully cut away the outer layer. Inside was a small plastic box with a screen and dials, something like a portable GPS.

"Why didn't they give us this thing in the first place?" Campbell asked.

"Because Whitlock and Young were at the ranch. The Big Kahuna thought we wouldn't have any trouble tracking them, but when they got away, we needed this extra piece of equipment." As he spoke, he flipped the on switch and waited for the machine to power up. When the screen was on, he moved the map function until a blinking circle appeared at the far right edge of the screen. By manipulating the controls, he was able to bring the circle closer to the center of the screen.

"They're right there." He pointed. "And they're not moving. It looks like they've bedded down for the evening."

"Okay."

"So we're heading for Rapid City."

"Now that we're got the general area, we can fine-tune the display and zero in on them."

Chapter Six

Shelley kept her angry gaze on Matt. "Allow me to make my own decisions."

His expression turned grim. "Didn't you hear what Jack and Claudia were telling us? This is dangerous. These people will kill to protect their own interests."

"I know that. And I know that my little boy is alone and scared and wanting his mommy. And if anybody can find him, I can."

She saw Matt's face contort.

"So don't try to send me away."

He swallowed. "I was…trying to keep you safe."

Her answer exploded from her. "I don't want to be *safe*. I want to find my son. That's why I came to you in the first place." She made an effort to rein in her fear and frustration. "This is like what you did five years ago. Making decisions for me. You sent me away because you thought it was the best thing for me. But it wasn't."

"Yeah, well, five years ago, you thought I was messed up. Which is why you left, never mind the 'push.' And since you came back, you've seen how paranoid I am."

When she started to object, he went on quickly. "And you saw how Jack acted. First he snuck up on us with a gun. Then he thought he heard something and rushed outside again. Guys like us aren't fit to be around," he growled.

She kept her gaze fixed on him. "You and Jack have good reason to behave the way you do. And you might have noticed that Claudia stuck with Jack when she could have left him. Don't use his behavior—or yours—as an excuse to get rid of me now. And don't use the danger either. The best chance of finding Trevor is if we work together."

As she saw his expression soften, she relaxed a little.

"Okay."

She kept her voice firm. "And don't try to use your powers on me again."

"I said okay," he snapped, and she knew she couldn't push him any farther. Instead, she tried to let him know she understood the fear and the frustration he was feeling.

"I realize you're used to making decisions on your own," she said in a gentler voice. "I mean since you came back from being kidnapped and saw your mom wasn't going to be much help."

"Yeah."

She swallowed and continued. "But now I believe that neither one of us can find Trevor alone."

His gaze bore into her. "Why?"

She spread her hands. "It's a feeling I have. Maybe I've got some powers, too. I've got the I gene."

"You never got any injections."

"There must be some kind of latent potential. They must have hoped for that in you."

"If what you're saying is true, then you're got more native ability than I do."

She shrugged. "It doesn't matter who's got what. Let's stop arguing about it and work together."

He nodded. "We should try to figure out our next move. Jack and Claudia gave us a lot of background. Unfortunately, they didn't tell us anything that was going to help us find Trevor. Not in practical terms."

"We could do research on those two guys—Dr. Sykes and Dr. Lasher," she suggested.

"Would that do any good? Lasher is dead and Sykes has gone underground."

She sighed. "What about contacting somebody at the Defense Department?"

"Do you think they'd admit to a secret project to make super soldiers? Especially when their chief researcher went rogue," he asked.

"Probably not."

He sighed too. "There may not be anyone in the DOD who even knows about the project. We may have to ask the FBI for help, since they got involved in the case."

"I'd like to sleep on that," she murmured. She'd come to Matt because the kidnappers had warned her not to go to the authorities. After talking to Jack and Claudia, she was almost sure that was just a ploy to keep her from any kind of effective search while they did their experiments on the "next generation" of children. But what if the kidnappers had meant what they said? What if she was putting Trevor's life in danger now?

As she remembered how Jack had run outside looking for someone sneaking up on the cabin, she felt a terrible restlessness that made her want to dash outside *this* cabin. Only she wouldn't be looking for men sneaking up on her and Matt. She'd be searching wildly around the parking lot and then in the pine forest beyond. Searching for her son. Which was a pretty crazy idea.

Matt had said he was messed up. Was she the one losing it now because she simply couldn't deal with their lack of progress today? Or her own uncertainty about what to do?

Trying to focus on something normal, she said, "We should get something to eat, then get some rest."

"Okay."

They drove into the center of town and stopped at a little deli, where they bought sandwiches and potato salad, which they took back to the room and ate at the table by the window. Neither one of them was very hungry, but she remembered what Matt had told her earlier. They needed to keep their strength up.

It was dark soon after five, and Matt took her advice and lay down on one of the double beds. Although he didn't look very relaxed, at least he was off his feet.

But she couldn't rid herself of her own fidgety restlessness. She kept feeling as though Trevor was calling her, and if she opened the door, she would see him in the parking lot of the motel.

Again, she told herself that was ridiculous. He couldn't be *here*. Somebody was holding him captive. And not outside a motel in Rapid City, South Dakota.

But Matt had been held captive, and he'd gotten away. Maybe Trevor had done the same thing, and now he was searching for his mommy.

Feeling like a sneak, she glanced back at Matt and saw that his eyes were closed. He needed to sleep, and she wasn't going to wake him up to tell him she was going outside. Or give him a chance to veto the move.

Quietly she pulled on her boots and coat before slipping outside. The South Dakota night was cold and crisp, and she stood for a moment on the porch of the cabin, not making a sound and staring out into the parking area. After her eyes were accustomed to the dark, she walked down the step to the blacktop that had been plowed free of snow.

Although she saw no one, she called softly, "Trevor?"

In answer, she thought she heard his voice, very faint and far away, and despite herself, she felt her heart leap.

"Trevor? Honey, it's Mommy. Are you here?"

When nobody answered, she walked across the parking area and into the snow under the trees, searching the darkness, still calling her son's name. "Tell me where you are, honey. I'll find you."

She was fifty yards from the cabin when footsteps behind her made her stop in her tracks. They were much too heavy for a little boy's.

Feeling trapped, she whirled.

It was Matt.

"What are you doing?" he asked.

She knew her face had gone hot and was glad he couldn't see the flare of heat in the darkness. "I'm looking for Trevor."

"He's not here."

She felt her insides contract. "If I go by logic, I know you're right, but I keep feeling like I'll step around a tree and there he'll be. Or if I can just look in the right direction, I'll see him standing there."

Matt came up behind her and put his arms around her, then turned her toward him, hugging her awkwardly in their bulky coats. "I know. I want him to be here, too. But I don't think he's just wandering around in the woods outside our motel."

Although she'd had a similar thought earlier, now she wanted to insist that she'd really and truly heard her son. But it didn't make any sense.

"It's cold out here. Come on back inside."

She wanted to scream at him to leave her alone. If she just stayed outside, she would find Trevor. Or would she?

"Am I going crazy?" she said in a small voice.

"Of course not! You just want to find him—very badly."

"Yes," she whispered, still not entirely convinced that he wasn't nearby. But she knew she couldn't stay out in the biting cold.

Shoulders slumped, she let Matt lead her back to the cabin.

"You should get some sleep."

"Okay," she answered without enthusiasm. If she could get to sleep, it would be a miracle.

She took a shower, washed her hair and dried it to give herself something to do. When she came back into the bedroom, Matt had turned off the lights. He was on the same bed where he'd been before, still dressed, except for his shoes, and he was lying on top of the covers.

As before, his eyes were closed, but she was sure he was aware of her every movement as she walked across the room, trying to decide which bed to climb into. It was tempting to lie down with him. He'd put his arm around her, and she'd draw some comfort from that. But would either one of them be able to stop themselves from going farther? She didn't want to find out.

OUTSIDE in the darkness, Bobby Savage and Don Campbell cruised down the highway.

"We're getting closer," Campbell said. He was the one holding the tracking device that had been shipped to a local freight office.

"Yeah."

"I think this is the place."

"No, I think it's the next motel down the road. Those cabins." Ignoring Campbell, Savage pulled into the motel parking lot and checked the screen. "Yeah, this is it."

"Which room?"

"This thing doesn't give room numbers! You've got to figure it out." He held up the GPS device. "We walk toward the cabins, and we'll be able to tell which is the right one."

Savage backed up their rental car onto the access road that led to the main parking lot, then cut the engine. They got out into the frigid night air. Campbell came around to the driver's side so they could both look at the screen.

"This way," Savage said as they started toward the row of cabins.

"They picked a pretty crummy place."

"Maybe they're running out of cash. Or they wanted a flop where the management wouldn't ask a lot of questions."

"So how do we work it?"

"We knock on the door. If they don't open up, we kick it in, grab them and split before anybody else knows we're here."

STILL HESITATING and still feeling that her son was somewhere nearby, Shelley walked to the window and lifted one of the slats. When a flash of movement caught her attention, she went very still, expecting to see Trevor. But it wasn't him. Instead, two men were striding up the access road that led to their cabin, and in the illumination from one of the parking lot lights, she saw the glint of metal.

They were carrying guns.

Turning from the window, she charged across the room to Matt's side and bent to tell him in a harsh whisper, "You have to get up."

Matt's eyes remained closed. "I'm sorry. He's not out there."

"It's not him. Two men are coming toward the cabin. They both have guns."

He swore and reached for the boots he'd left beside the bed. Quickly he pulled them on.

While she shrugged on her coat, he inched the blinds aside, looked out and swore again.

"They're closing in pretty fast."

"What are we going to do?"

"Go out the bathroom window."

She looked at the travel bags that still sat on one of the chairs and the desk.

"Leave them."

Her heart was pounding as he hurried her into the bathroom and closed the lid on the toilet, then reached to open the small window above the tank. It wouldn't budge.

Muttering under his breath, he put his shoulder into the effort and managed to push the sash up as far as it would go.

It wasn't a very large opening, but cold air rushed into the bathroom, obliterating the warmth from her shower.

"Climb on the tank and get out," he said as he closed and locked the bathroom door. "Then head for the woods where you were before."

"What about you?"

"I'll be there in a minute."

She climbed onto the toilet seat, then onto the tank and stuck one leg out the window. By ducking low, she was able to maneuver her shoulders out.

When she looked down, she saw it was a six foot drop to the ground below. Just as she eased over the sill, she heard a knock on the door and froze.

Matt put a hand on her leg and pushed. "Go! If you hear gunshots, don't worry."

She gasped. "What do you mean don't worry?"

"I'm going to give them an order to make some noise. But you've got to get away first."

She didn't want to leave him, but when she heard another loud rap at the door, she made herself drop down to the ground in back of the cabin, the snow cushioning her fall.

Matt had told her to run into the woods, but she couldn't do it until she knew he was out of the room.

When he stuck his head out and saw she was still there, he made an angry sound. "Go on. I'll catch up with you."

With no other option, she ran toward the pine trees, seeing her previous tracks in the snow. Crossing and recrossing them, she hoped that would confuse the men when they came looking for her and Matt.

MATT DASHED BACK into the bedroom. He could hear the men on the other side of the door, and he'd gotten a quick look at them, which should help.

Step away from the door, he silently ordered. *You want to step away from the door and into the parking lot. Pull your guns and start shooting into the air.*

He repeated the suggestion, then waited with his breath frozen in his lungs, listening for some sound from outside the cabin.

For centuries, nothing happened. Finally, when he heard shuffling feet, he figured they were going back to the parking lot, but that wasn't the most important part of his directions. He needed a disturbance that would wake up the motel owners and bring the cops swooping in.

Pull your guns, and start shooting, he ordered again. *Shoot into the air, so nobody gets hurt.*

Again he waited for an eternity, and he started wondering if he should head for the bathroom window before he knew the outcome of his ploy. Then the sound of an automatic pistol split the air.

"Good going." He wasn't sure whether he was talking to the would-be assailants or himself. Either way, it had worked.

Outside, more shots broke the silence of the winter night, and he could hear the men cursing at each other.

"What the hell are you doing?

"What do you mean me? You started it."

"You did."

After a second's hesitation, Matt gathered up the travel bags and dashed back across the room. Climbing onto the toilet tank, he tossed the bags out the window, then threw his leg over the sill. He was bigger than Shelley, and it was a little harder to get his shoulders through the opening, but he managed to wiggle out, then dropped to the ground. As he reached for the bags, he saw Shelley's tracks leading along the back of the cabin to the woods where he'd found her earlier. Well, more than one set of tracks. She must have tried to confuse the pursuers by crossing and re-crossing her path. The trouble was, she was confusing him, too.

In the distance, he could hear police sirens wailing, and he knew that his trick had worked. At least in the short run.

The cops were on their way.

Peering around the side of the cabin, he saw the two men running down the driveway, which left him and Shelley to explain who had been shooting up a peaceful motel.

"Shelley?" he called softly, but she didn't answer.

Hoping she was in the woods, he headed in that direction, but he couldn't tell which way she had gone. Not with the confusion of trails she'd left.

He wanted to shout out louder, but that might bring the men running back up the driveway to…

To what?

Kill them? Capture them? He didn't even know who they were, what they wanted or who had sent them. But he had to assume that it had something to do with the conspiracy that had snagged him—and Trevor.

Knowing they were running out of time, he hurried farther into the darkness under the trees, calling softly again.

Movement to his right made him stiffen. When Shelley stepped out from behind a tree, he sighed in relief.

"Come on."

"Where?"

"I don't know. But we have to get away before the cops arrive and start asking questions."

"Okay."

They hurried back to the parking area, but it was already too late. A patrol car had pulled up in front of their cabin, and two cops jumped out.

Matt cursed under his breath.

"How do they know which unit?"

"I guess someone saw the bad guys knocking at the door."

The patrol officers also knocked. "Police. Open up."

When nobody answered, the cops started around the cabin, one going right and one going left.

"They'll see our tracks and try to follow the trail," he said. "We'll make our move when they're both in back."

He took her arm, feeling her tension. He'd used his power to get the two men to start shooting. Could he use it on the law? Once again, he knew he had to try.

Stay in back of the cabin, he silently ordered. *Stay back there for a few minutes, looking around. Stay in back of the cabin. Try to figure out what's going on with that mass of footprints.*

"Are you using your powers?" Shelley whispered.

"How do you know?"

"By your expression. You look like you're trying to push a steel spike through a stone wall."

That was about how it felt. "Yeah."

He waited a few beats, then said, "Now."

They both rushed out of the woods, and he unlocked both car doors. "Get into the driver's seat," he told Shelley.

"What are you going to do?"

"Give the car a push, so we don't have to start the engine and alert them."

She climbed behind the wheel, and he threw the travel bags in the back, then hesitated again.

How much time did they have?

Taking a chance, he ran to the patrol car, opened the door and sprang the hood release. Then he lifted the hood and pulled out a spark plug, which he put in his pocket. After lowering the hood he dashed back to the rental car and started to push, expecting every moment that the law officers would come rushing back into the parking area and discovering what he was doing.

Would they yell, "Stop. Police," then start shooting? He hoped he didn't end up with a bullet in his back.

At least he had gravity on his side. The cabin was at the top of a hill, and he got the car rolling, then had to dash after it to reach the passenger door and jump inside. But he made it as the car picked up speed.

"Thank God. Can I start the engine?" Shelley asked.

"Yes."

She turned the key and nothing happened.

"Start the car!"

"I'm trying. Maybe it's cold."

He was debating whether to try and change seats with her when he heard a shout behind him.

"Stop. Police."

He wanted to curse. Instead he kept his voice even. "Just relax. Turn the key again, and give it some gas."

She did, and the engine finally turned over.

Twisting around, he watched the cops leap into their cruiser. But the ploy with the spark plug had worked, and the vehicle stayed where it was.

"Get the hell out of here," he told Shelley. "And pray that there's not another patrol car in the area."

She winced and turned right when they reached the access road to the highway.

When they saw a police cruiser racing toward them with lights flashing and siren blasting, she made a choking sound. "What should I do?"

"Keep going. They don't know who we are. I hope," he added under his breath.

The cruiser rushed by, and they continued up the highway as though they'd just been out getting groceries or something.

"Get off at the next exit," he said. "Then stop after you've made the turn, and I'll drive."

She did as he asked, and they switched places. He drove at a normal speed, then took a side road into a residential area, where he made several more turns, looking to see if they were being followed.

Shelley's features were rigid. "The authorities will think we did it. I mean, shooting up the parking lot."

"True, but they don't know who they're looking for. I registered under a fake name and paid cash. Our main problem is the bad guys."

"I don't like breaking the law."

He swiveled toward her. "You want to spend a bunch of time explaining what's going on?"

She swallowed. "No."

Still weaving through the residential area, he headed toward the tourist district. "Make sure nobody is behind us."

"Okay." She twisted around in her seat, looking out the back window. "Where did those men go when they left?"

"I don't know."

"Maybe the cops will find them."

"We can hope."

She turned back toward him, her face rigid with worry. "How did the bad guys find us?"

He made an angry sound. "I'm working on that. They didn't show up at our cabin by accident. So they must have had some inside information."

"Jack and Claudia didn't tell them," she said in a firm voice. "Even if they wanted to rat us out, they didn't know where we were."

"I guess that's right."

"What about your credit card?"

"I had to use it to get a rental car. But, like I said, I didn't use one at the motel. And they didn't have a transponder on our car, because it's a rental."

"What's a transponder?"

"A signal device that would let somebody find a particular moving object." He made an angry sound. "So if there is one, the only possibility is that it's on *me*."

She gasped. "What do you mean?"

"Somewhere under my skin there's a tracking device, and we have to get it out before those guys can zero in on the signal again."

"You're making a big assumption."

"What else could it be?"

"I don't know." She clenched her fists on her lap. "They could have been checking every motel in the area—looking for the car you rented."

"That's a possibility—but a pretty long shot, since it would take a lot of manpower. I think we have to go with the transponder theory." He thought about the best plan of action. "We'll head for Ellsworth Air Force Base. They might have some electronics equipment up there that would jam the signal. And there will be plenty of motels."

"We're going to stay there?"

"Briefly."

As HE DROVE, Bobby Savage turned to his partner. "Are you picking him up again?"

"Partially," Don Campbell answered.

"What do you mean?"

"The screen's not stable. It's flashing in and out. Something must be getting in the way of the transmission."

"Like what?"

"How the hell do I know? I've never used one of these things before. I think we're getting closer. We just have to hope that the signal gets stronger and homes in on them."

Neither one of them mentioned the incident in the parking lot, where they'd started shooting into the air like a couple of drunken cowboys.

Neither one of them wanted to admit that something strange had happened. At least now they were heading in the right direction. That was the important point.

AFTER MAKING SURE there was no car sticking to their tail, Matt turned onto Highway 90 and headed east toward the base. As he'd predicted, there were lots of motels.

Before getting a room, he pulled into the parking lot of a drugstore.

"What are you doing?"

"Getting some things we're going to need. You stay in the car, so we won't be seen together in there. I'll be back as quickly as I can."

She slumped down in the seat, and he went inside, heading for the back of the store, where he bought alcohol, gauze, tape and tweezers. He also got a baseball hat with the logo of a local team and a pair of sunglasses.

After paying for his purchases, he climbed back into the car.

"I don't like this," Shelley murmured.

"Of course not." He turned onto a road near the base that was lined with bars, motels and pawnshops.

"Look for a motel where the lights in the parking lot are dim and there aren't a lot of cars."

"Okay." She leaned forward, watching the passing scenery, then called out. "There's one."

"Good."

He turned in and cut the engine, then pulled the baseball cap and sunglasses out of the drugstore bag.

"How do I look?"

"Kind of strange. Who wears sunglasses at night?"

"Guys who don't want to be recognized. Wait here."

Once again, she slumped down in her seat as he walked into the dingy office.

"Can I get a room for a few hours?" he asked a short young man who was watching a wrestling match on a small television screen behind the counter.

The guy looked up, studying him. "You can, but it will cost you the same as all night."

He glanced back toward the car. "I'm with a lady who doesn't want her husband to find out where she is."

"Uh-huh."

He wanted this to work. Could he give them some extra insurance? You like me. *You want to help me out. You won't tell anyone that you've seen me.* He silently sent that message to the clerk, then repeated the instructions aloud.

"If a guy comes looking for us, tell him you haven't registered anyone in the last couple of hours."

The clerk hesitated.

"There's something in it for you." As he got out his wallet, he added a fifty-dollar tip as insurance. "I'd like a room as close to the end of the row as possible."

"Okay," the clerk agreed, although Matt wasn't absolutely sure the guy was going to keep his mouth shut.

But they did get the end unit, and Matt was able to pull around the corner and leave the car in the shadows.

As soon as they stepped into the room, he closed the drapes, then turned to Shelley.

"We're going to try and find that transponder. You're going to have to help me."

She looked uncertain.

"I can do part of it. But there are places on my body that I can't see."

"You're serious about this."

"Yeah. And we'd better hurry. Because if the thing is active and there's no interference from the air base, we have to get it out of me and get out of here before those guys come after us again."

She shuddered.

He turned on all the lights, wishing the room were brighter, then started taking off his clothing. When he had stripped to his shorts, he sat down on the side of the bed. "We'll start at the top with my scalp and work our way down."

Slowly, he began to run his hands through his hair, trying to feel every inch of his scalp.

"I should help you," she said, sitting down beside him.

"Yeah."

She began to work her fingers through his hair, and he closed his eyes, enjoying her touch, even though he knew that their purpose was serious.

"Nothing here, I think, although I don't exactly know what I'm looking for."

"Neither do I, but I assume we'll recognize it when we find it. See if there's a place where my skin seems a little raised. Or a little firm. If it's not in my hair, we'll look for raised places and discoloration."

She went on to his neck and his ears, carefully running her fingers over every inch of his skin. Then she started on his shoulders.

"I guess I should lie down," he said in a husky voice.

"Yes."

He would have liked to give in to the sensuality of her touch, but he kept thinking that the bad guys could come bursting through the door at any second. And they'd find him almost naked.

To speed up the process, he searched his chest, stomach and sides, while she did his arms. Then he turned over, and she ran her hands over his back.

His feet and legs were next. He did the right side. She did the left.

"Nothing," she said when she'd examined everything from his toes to his thighs. "I guess you're wrong."

"We haven't finished."

"Matt, you don't think they could put something *there?*"

"You want to take a chance on it?" he asked, reaching for the waistband of his shorts.

"Okay. No."

After he was entirely naked, he turned over on his stomach.

"I guess you've got to search my butt."

"Is this some new sex game?"

"I wish."

He heard her swallow, then felt her hands on him.

After a few moments, she said, "Just the usual hairy male cheeks."

"There are only a couple of places left."

Heaving himself onto his back, he stacked his hands behind his head and tried to act like he felt comfortable as she stared down at his genitals.

"You've probably seen a naked man before," he quipped.

"Right. You."

"Nobody else?"

She didn't meet his eyes. "I'm not very…experienced," she whispered.

He felt his heart turn over. Was she saying he was the only man she'd made love with? He wanted to ask, but he knew this wasn't the time or the place.

With a jerky motion, she reached out, connecting with his most intimate area, running her hands over it.

He lay with his eyes closed and his hands flat on the bedspread, willing himself not to let her touch turn him on.

The old trick of saying the multiplication tables helped. But Shelley's attentions were erotic, even when she was doing something perfectly innocent, and he was relieved when she went on to his inner thigh.

When she reached a spot high up in his groin, she made a small sound.

"What?"

"I think I feel something."

He sat up, looked down, and stared at the spot she was pointing to.

There was a slightly raised place that he'd always thought was a mole, but as he eyed it now and prodded it with his finger, he was pretty sure the darkened color was coming from something under the skin, not from the surface.

"I think that's it," he muttered.
"What are we going to do?"
"Take it out."

Chapter Seven

Shelley's eyes widened as she stared at Matt. "You're kidding, right?"

He shook his head. "No. I'm deadly serious. If that's a transponder, those men used it to find me, and they can do it again. It has to come out, because they're probably on their way here right now."

"What if it's not a...transponder."

"Then I'll be putting myself through a little unnecessary pain."

"I don't like the sound of that."

"I don't think we have a choice."

Without giving her the opportunity to argue further, he climbed off the bed, disappeared into the bathroom, and came back with a couple of towels. Then he pulled a penknife out of his pocket.

As she watched in a kind of dumb shock, he took out a bottle of alcohol he'd bought at the drugstore and poured it over the blade of his knife, then did the same thing with a pair of tweezers he'd also bought.

After laying them on a piece of sterile gauze, he used another piece of gauze to wipe the skin over the bump he'd found. When he'd finished, he put one towel under himself and used the other to drape his genitals.

"Look out the window and make sure no cars are pulling up in front of our room," he said. "I don't want to get caught in the middle of this."

Glad of the excuse to turn away from him—and to postpone what she knew was coming—she went to the window and pulled the drapes aside. When she looked out, she saw no one.

"Nobody out there," she said.

"Then wash your hands so we can get this over with."

Numbly, she did as he asked, but when she came back to him, she could hardly breathe around the lump in her throat.

"I can't," she whispered.

His face took on a look of resignation. "You want me to sit up and try and dig it out? That's going to be a little convoluted, but I'll take a whack at it."

The word *whack* made her suck in a sharp breath. "No!"

"Then pretend you're taking a splinter out of Trevor."

"An unlikely place for a splinter," she muttered.

"Unfortunately." He lay back and closed his eyes.

Hating her choices, she eased onto the bed beside him and took the knife.

Please God, let me do this fast and keep my hands steady, she silently prayed as she bent toward the place she'd found. Knowing she was going to hurt him, she pressed the knife against his flesh, but not hard enough to penetrate.

"Do it! The sooner you get it over with, the better for both of us," he said.

When she looked up at him, his teeth were clenched.

Praying that she had the strength to see this through, she pushed the point of the knife through his skin, feeling his body go rigid as she began to probe for the foreign body.

When the point of the knife hit something hard, he made a low sound. "I guess there's more there than a freckle."

"Yes." She changed the angle, digging under it, working as fast as she could without damaging too much of his flesh.

After pushing the thing toward the surface, she used the tweezers to grasp the edge and pull.

A small metal rectangle came free. Sitting up, Matt looked at it the way he might look at a tick he'd taken off a dog.

"SOMETHING STRANGE," Bobby Savage growled.

"Now what?"

"The screen just blipped."

"That interference again?"

"I don't know. We'd better hurry up before the system goes down or something."

"Okay. There's a motel up ahead. I think that's it." He checked the screen. "Yeah. We got them cornered." He looked at his partner. "And this time no shooting."

"Yeah."

He turned in at the motel sign and stopped at the edge of the parking lot, looking at the screen and trying to figure out exactly which unit they wanted. It seemed to be down by the end, but there were lights on in a couple of the windows down there, and he couldn't be sure until they got out of the car.

"I...I GUESS you were right," Shelley whispered.

"Yeah," Matt answered between clenched teeth. Taking the flat metal disk from her, he used the tweezers to crumple it.

"I'd like to take it to the FBI, but I think we'd better flush it down the toilet," he said in a gritty voice. "In case it can still function."

"Yes." Looking at it with disgust, she carried it into the bathroom and dropped it in the toilet bowl. After flushing, she watched to make sure that it had actually gone down the drain.

When she returned to the bedroom, Matt was swabbing more alcohol on the spot she'd cut. Next, he taped on a couple of gauze pads.

"I hurt you," she whispered, struggling to control her emotions. Now that she was finished with the operation, she had to press her hands against her hips to keep them from shaking.

"We had to get rid of that thing." Reaching for his pants, he started getting dressed.

She watched in disbelief. "You just had an operation. You should lie down."

"Not yet. It's not safe. We have to get out of here while we still can."

"Why?"

"Because that thing was giving off a signal until a few minutes ago. Anyone following the trail could end up at this motel and start looking through the rooms."

When he continued getting dressed, she pulled on her coat, then watched as he eased the curtains aside again.

"Damn!"

"What?"

"I think we're already too late. I believe those bastards are in the parking lot. They traced me this far before the signal went dead. It looks like they were right behind us!"

Her heart leaped into her throat. "How do you know it's them? It could be someone who wants to spend the night."

"I don't think so. It looks like the same car as before."

"What are we going to do?" she asked in a voice she couldn't quite hold steady.

"Let's see what happens."

The driver of the vehicle hesitated for several moments, then drove into the lot and pulled up at the office, where a man got out and walked toward the vacancy sign.

When he went inside, Matt waited a few moments. "I told the clerk I was getting a room with another man's wife."

She winced.

"I paid him extra to say nobody had checked in during the

past few hours. You slip out the door and walk around the corner to the car. Stay in the shadows, close to the wall."

"What about you?"

"I'll wait thirty seconds and follow you."

Her heart was thumping as she opened the door a crack, inched out and walked rapidly along the wall toward the corner of the building.

Ignoring the impulse to look back around the corner, she opened the car door, climbed inside and sat waiting tensely for Matt to follow her.

As promised, he showed up thirty seconds later and slipped behind the wheel.

BOBBY SAVAGE resisted the urge to grab the clerk by the collar and slam his face against the counter a couple of times.

"Nobody's checked in in the past hour?" he asked.

"No."

"Nobody paid you to say that?"

The man hesitated.

"There's a hundred dollars in it if you tell me where he is."

There was a long pause. "You the husband?"

"What?"

"He said he was having a quickie with another guy's wife."

"That so? Yeah. I'm the husband." He took out a hundred-dollar bill and slapped it on the counter.

"Last room on the right."

"Thanks, buddy." Bobby turned back toward the door, just as a car that had been hidden around the side of the building pulled out of the lot.

He hesitated. That could be them. Or they could still be in the room.

"SO FAR, so good," Matt murmured.

They drove along the far edge of the lot, past the car that

was parked at the office. Nobody followed them as they turned onto the highway.

She looked behind them, but the car they'd seen was still at the office.

"I think we got away."

"Yeah. Finally a lucky break, but we'd better put some distance between this place and us, since the motel was the last known location of the transponder."

"You're not staying near the air base?"

"If those guys are desperate to find us, they could check every motel, and the next clerk might not let me pay him to say we're not there. Or he might call the police if I seem suspicious."

She answered with a tight nod.

"We'll head back toward Rapid City, then keep going down the highway to the other side of town."

They drove into the night.

When she glanced at Matt, his features were set.

"Does that place on your thigh hurt?" she murmured.

"I'm fine."

"You had that thing in you for years, but they didn't use it until you went looking for Trevor and they lost your trail."

"Yeah."

"That was gutsy of you to have me dig that thing out of you," she whispered.

"I don't think I had a choice. If it was under your skin, you would have done it—if it was the only way to make sure those goons stopped following us."

"Yes," she answered.

She wanted to reach out and press her palm over Matt's hand, because she needed the contact, but she didn't want to distract him.

"Every time I think it can't get worse, it does," she whispered.

"Yeah."

"Maybe we do have to call the FBI."

"In the morning. If we still think it's a good idea."

She leaned back and closed her eyes, and somehow she must have fallen asleep, because the next thing she knew, Matt was pulling into another parking lot.

Blinking, she sat up. "Where are we?"

"Another motel. On the other side of Rapid City. I'll be right back."

She peered at the establishment, which looked a lot more upscale than the last place they'd been.

Matt was back in a few minutes with the key to their room.

"Aren't you going to run out of cash?" she asked.

"I keep a fair amount at the ranch. It's not going to be a problem for a while."

As they walked to the room, she didn't ask how long "a while" would be, because she didn't want to think that they might be out here for weeks searching for Trevor. When she'd come to Matt for help, she'd had no idea of what finding her son was really going to entail—or how much danger they would be in. Or how much she needed Matt. She never could have gotten this far without him.

He unlocked the door, and she stepped into a sitting area, with two doors.

"What's this?" she asked in confusion as he closed the outside door behind them.

"I thought you might want to have your own room," he answered in a gritty voice.

After everything that had happened today, that was the last thing she wanted, but she couldn't make herself admit that to him, not after the way she'd carried on this morning.

Silently, she picked up the bag he'd set down and stepped to the right. Opening the door, she found a comfortable-looking room with a queen-sized bed.

Behind her, the door to the other room closed, and she flinched, feeling as if Matt was pushing her away. Then she reminded herself that she was the one who had tried to put some distance between them this morning.

She needed to sleep, she told herself as she crossed to the bed and pulled back the covers. But she didn't lie down.

Without giving herself time to change her mind, she reversed direction, walked out of her room and across the small space that separated her from Matt. Raising her hand, she knocked on the door.

Moments later, Matt was looking at her questioningly. He'd gotten undressed and was wearing only briefs and a T-shirt.

"A while ago, I hurt you," she said, her eyes going to the bandage on his right thigh. "I was thinking that I could make it up by giving you a massage."

He hesitated for several seconds, and she thought he was going to do what he believed was right—not what he wanted. "You're sure?" he finally asked.

"Yes."

Stepping into the room, she closed the door behind her.

"I guess you should, you know, pull back the spread and blanket and lie down," she said. "And take off your shirt."

"Okay."

He pulled back the covers, then stretched out face down.

"I'll be right back."

In the bathroom she grabbed the small bottle of hand lotion from the tray of toiletries, then came back into the bedroom, where he was lying with his eyes closed and his head resting on his folded arms.

After a few seconds hesitation, she climbed onto the bed, straddling Matt's hips. He stayed very still as she poured some of the lotion and began to work at the tense muscles of his neck and shoulders

"That's good," he murmured.

She kept working on him with slick hands, trying not to admit that straddling him and touching him were turning her on. That wasn't what she'd intended, she told herself. She'd only wanted to be close to him, and this was an excellent way to do it.

To distract herself from the physical sensations, she said, "You think they put the transponder in you when they kidnapped you?"

"Yes."

"Did Jack Maddox have one?"

"I don't know."

"Why would they treat different prisoners differently?"

Matt hesitated before speaking. "They had him for a long time, and maybe thought he was never going to get away. So they didn't bother tagging him."

"That's horrible."

"Tell me about it."

The next question made her throat tighten. "You think they planned to let you go?"

"Release me back into the general population?" He laughed harshly. "I don't know. Maybe they had a long-term program for him and they only planned to have me for a few months so they could do a few fun experiments."

"Fun!"

"For them."

"What did they want to accomplish with you?"

"I wish I knew. It could be that they wanted to study the I gene in more people. Or it could be that I was a disappointment to them. Maybe I couldn't do what they wanted with my mind, so they decided to cut their losses."

"If that's true, thank God."

"In this case, maybe it's better to be a failure."

"You're not a failure! You stopped those men from capturing or killing us."

He was silent for several moments, then said, "The power increased as I got older. Maybe they don't know that." He sighed and went on. "Or maybe they've kept tabs on me all along. I mean, they could have planted a ranch hand at the Silver Stallion."

"You have anybody in mind?"

"Not really. But for years I felt like somebody was watching me. Maybe they were trying to judge how well I was using my talent."

"That's horrible!"

"Agreed."

She kept massaging him, but the conversation had made her think about Trevor again, and Matt must have sensed a change in her touch.

"Shelley?"

"I…" When she swallowed a sob, he turned over and pulled her down so that she was cradled against his chest.

"Oh, sweetheart. I was running my mouth, and you were applying all that to your son, weren't you."

Still struggling not to cry, she could only nod.

"It's okay to let yourself go," he whispered as he stroked his hands over her arms and through her hair. "We've had a hell of a day."

"You never let go."

"I'm a guy. Guys have to be stoic."

She closed her eyes and pressed her forehead against his chest. "Everything that happens makes me worry about Trevor. About the kind of people who have him."

"I'm worried about him, too. And at the same time I understand that the two of us have to keep ourselves safe and sane, because we're the only people who can rescue him."

"I know that's true, but I feel so confused and guilty. Trevor is missing, and he's the only thing I should be focused on. But then I want you to take me away from worrying about him—just for a little while."

He raised his head and looked down at her. "Are you saying that I don't have to feel guilty that the whole time you were looking for that transponder, I was trying my damnedest not to get turned on? I knew you were searching for a piece of spy equipment, but your hands on me made every nerve ending in my body tingle with pleasure. That's how bad off I am."

She swallowed. "It was the same for me. Touching you all over made me want you. And then…" She couldn't hold back a little sob. "And then I had to stick a knife in you. In a very sensitive place."

"I made you do it."

"It was horrible."

"I'm so sorry for that, but there wasn't any other way. Those guys showed up before we left the motel."

"Yes." She felt her throat tighten. "Make me forget about all the bad stuff. Just for a while."

"You know what you're asking?"

"Yes."

Cupping the back of his head, she brought his mouth to hers for a kiss that started off sweet and quickly turned erotic.

Heat flared between them as he gathered her close, pressing her center to his erection.

"Oh!"

"You're not the only one who feels guilty."

"Don't say that! Don't tell me this is wrong. Maybe it's the only thing that can give me the strength to keep going," she whispered.

"I was trying to be strong—and not reach for you."

"Don't be strong." She breathed his name as she stroked her lips against his jaw, then slid lower, caressing the column of his neck, nibbling with her teeth, then feathering kisses on his collarbone.

Pleased with his response, she whispered against his heated skin, "We need each other tonight."

Keeping his gaze on her face, he slid his hands under her shirt, stroking her back. She pulled her T-shirt over her head and tossed it onto the floor along with her bra before she came back to nestle beside him again.

"That's a beautiful view," he said as he stared down at her. "But up close will be even better." Lowering his head, he buried his face between her breasts, turning one way and then the other before closing his lips around one of her hardened nipples.

His thumb and finger closed around her other nipple, squeezing and pulling as he suckled her.

"Oh." He was turning her molten, using all his knowledge of her responses to transport her to a world of pure sensation.

After one last taste of her breast, he shifted his position, kissing his way downward to the waistband of her jeans, where he undid the snap and lowered the zipper before pushing the fabric aside with his face.

Slowly, he eased his hand inside her panties, playing with the crinkly hair he encountered, then gliding lower to slip into her slick folds.

She couldn't hold back a cry of pleasure, lifting her hips toward his questing fingers. Watching her face, he dipped his finger inside her, then slid it up to her most sensitive flesh.

"You're going to push me over the edge," she gasped, reaching down to still his hand. "Don't do that yet. I want to make this last."

She took both his hands in hers, folding them over so she could kiss his knuckles.

"Tell me what you want," he said in a husky voice. "Anything in my power."

"I'll show you."

She moved away from him, taking off her jeans and panties, then lay on her side, staring at him. Very lightly she reached out to graze his shoulder, his chest, keeping her touch feathery. She had run her fingers over him earlier, looking for the transponder, and they had both been turned on, although neither one of them had admitted it.

Now her intent was purely sexual, and they both knew it. She could see exactly the effect she was having on him, as she skimmed down to his belly, then skipped his sex and played with his thighs.

The sound of his labored breathing set her pulse pounding, and she wanted to pull his body back against hers. But she forced herself to stay where she was, drawing out the pleasure until they were both tingling with need.

When she knew neither one of them could wait another second, she made her move.

"Lie on your back."

Climbing on top of him, she brought him inside her in one swift motion, then went still as she stared down at him.

"Shelley, that's so good."

"Yes."

She thrust her breasts toward him, lifting them in her hands, playing her fingers over her own nipples, knowing he was watching with greedy intensity.

Then, when it was impossible to stay still a second longer, she began to move her hips, raising and lowering herself, driving them both to the point of no return.

Leaning forward, she pressed her center against him, giving herself the pleasure of that intimate contact.

And when her inner muscles began to contract, he surged upward, both of them reaching the peak of ecstasy at the same time.

When she collapsed on top of him, he gathered her close and cradled her against his body.

She kissed his damp neck, snuggling against him.

"Don't turn against me in the morning," he whispered.

"I won't. I promise."

"Try to sleep. Tomorrow we'll decide our next move."

SHE DID SLEEP, soundly at first. Then a dream grabbed her. Once again, Trevor was calling to her.

"Mommy? Where are you, Mommy. I need you."

In the dream, she sat up and looked around. "Honey, you sound like you're right here. Where are you?"

"In a cabin."

"Where?"

"I don't know. Mommy, I'm scared."

Her heart squeezed painfully. "I know, honey. I know. Look around you, so I can see what you're seeing."

"Can you do that?"

"I don't know. I'm going to try."

She kept her eyes closed and let the vision come. She saw a small room. A narrow bed. Rough walls. A window. Outside was darkness.

"Can you see it?"

"I think so. The walls are rough wood planks, right?"

"Yes."

"And your bed has a brown blanket."

"Yes!"

"What's happening to you?"

"A mean man has me."

She gasped. "What is he doing to you?"

"He sticks needles in me. And he tells me to shut up when I cry."

She winced. "Oh, honey, I'm so sorry."

"I'm trying to be a big boy."

"I know. You are a big boy. If that man had me, I'd cry, too. But it's good that you can talk to me."

"Most boys can't do it, I think."

"I know. And you don't want to tell the man about it. Promise you'll keep this just between us."

"I promise."

"Good. Can you tell me the man's name?"

"Blue."

"His first name or his last name?"

"I don't know."

She tried to think of something that would help her.

"Does he talk on the phone to anyone?"

"I think so. But he only does it while I'm in the bedroom and he's in the other room."

"And he's not hurting you—except for the needles."

"He puts this handcuff around my wrist. Like the police have. But they wouldn't chain anybody to a bed, would they?"

"No!" Anger flared, but she tried to keep it out of her voice. "I'll take it off as soon as I get there. I'll be there to get you. I promise." She dragged in a breath and let it out. "Remember, it's important not to let the man know you talked to me."

"Okay."

"Don't forget. It's got to be our secret."

"Okay." His breath hitched "Mommy…"

"What?"

"He's coming back. I have to stop talking now."

"Trevor, wait."

"He'll catch me."

Just like that, the contact snapped and she was left shaking in frustration.

When she felt a hand on her shoulder, she gasped.

"Shelley, wake up. You're having a bad dream."

Her eyes blinked open. In the light from the bathroom, she saw Matt's worried face.

"What is it? What happened?"

"I talked to Trevor."

"You dreamed it."

She sat up and ran her hand through her hair. "I know it was a dream, but I think it was real, too."

"Okay."

"Do you believe me?"

"I want to. But I don't have enough information. What happened?"

"Trevor called to me—and then I was talking to him. He was in a bedroom in a cabin, with rough walls. The blanket on his bed was brown. The scene was very detailed. More detailed than any dream I've ever had."

"Okay."

"He says a man named Blue is holding him. That's a weird name, don't you think?"

"Yes."

Her breath hitched. "He says the man is sticking needles in him. Like you said happened to you. I didn't bring that up. He did."

"Yeah, but you know that from what I said."

She answered with a tight nod, then insisted, "I think it's real."

"Is there anything that would help us find Trevor?"

She closed her eyes, then flapped her arms in frustration. "I don't think so. But at least I know he's alive—and okay. I mean basically okay."

"Umm-hmm."

"You don't believe me," she said in a small voice

"How would it happen?"

An answer came to her. "The shots gave you a special power. And the same thing was true with Jack. Remember he asked, 'What's your power'?"

"Okay."

"Jack can sometimes see the future. You can give people a push. What if...what if those shots are giving Trevor the power to reach out to me? Get in contact in a way that's paranormal. And I can talk to him because I have the I gene too."

"That could be possible."

"Maybe there's a way to use that...to find him."

Matt made a rough sound. "That would turn the tables on those bastards."

"I hope so. I hope we can use their experiment against them to find Trevor."

His arm tightened around her. "I'd like that."

"I wanted to tell him his daddy was with me. And we'd find him together."

Matt sucked in a sharp breath. "I'd like him to know that I'm looking for him, too. But I think we don't want to introduce any new factors—yet."

"I know. That's what I was thinking." She moved restlessly beside him. "Maybe if I go back to sleep, I can talk to him again."

Feeling better than she had in days, she settled down beside Matt, and he clasped her close. It was comforting to feel his arm around her. Finally, she did fall asleep, hoping to speak to her son again.

Chapter Eight

Shelley fought disorientation as she woke. She wasn't in her own bed at home. And she wasn't...

At the ranch. Turning her head, she saw Matt lying next to her. They were at a motel he'd checked them into the night before. The third place they'd been. After the last motel, where she'd taken that horrible transponder out of his thigh.

That would have been enough for one night, but a lot had happened since then. Like making love with Matt—then dreaming that she was talking to Trevor.

Matt turned his head and gave her a critical inspection. "How do you feel?"

His face was tense. So was his voice, and she knew he was waiting for her to start explaining that they'd made a mistake last night, but she wasn't going to do it, not when she'd practically come in here with seduction in mind.

"Okay," she whispered instead.

Under the covers he reached for her hand and wrapped his fingers around hers. "Did you talk to Trevor again?"

Before she spoke, she shifted her hand so that her fingers were knitted with his. "No. Maybe I just dreamed the whole thing."

"I don't think so."

"You were skeptical when I first told you. Why not now?" she asked in a small voice.

"Because I've had time to think about how detailed and vivid it was. I'll bet when we find him, you'll see the same things you described."

"You really think so?"

"I wouldn't have said it otherwise."

"It could just be wishful thinking."

He rolled toward her and gathered her close. "Don't try to talk yourself out of it."

"Why not?"

"I think we have to assume that nothing connected with Trevor's disappearance is 'usual.' If you think you're able to talk to him, you probably can."

She raised her head and stared at Matt. "Even if it's true, he's just a little boy. He doesn't know where he is, and he doesn't know how to get away. Especially if he's chained to a bed."

Matt winced. "I know that's hard to take. But it tells us something, actually. I was in a secure facility. Somewhere they thought I couldn't get away. This guy Blue must have Trevor in a place where he could escape if he were free to run around the cabin. Or if someone could come scoop him up."

She felt a spurt of hope. "That's something."

He dragged in a breath and let it out before saying, "But it's not enough. I think we're at the point where we need some help."

She gulped. "You mean the FBI? That's taking a big chance—since the kidnappers warned me not to contact the authorities."

"We followed up our only lead. Do you have any other suggestions?"

"Maybe I can reach out to Trevor again," she said, searching Matt's face for some reaction. But he kept his features even.

"Okay. Do you want me to leave you alone?"

"Would you mind?"

"I'll go in the other bedroom. There's a bathroom in there where I can shower and get dressed. Then I'll get us some breakfast."

"I feel like I'm driving you away."

"Of course not. I'm just giving you some privacy. What do you want to eat?"

"Anything."

"The hotel has a breakfast bar. I'll get us something from down there. The less I'm outside, the better."

Her stomach knotted. "You mean because those men are still looking for us?"

"Yeah. I'm thinking they're not going to just give up, even without the transponder."

When he'd left the room, she plumped up the pillow, lay back and closed her eyes. She pictured the room that she'd seen and Trevor lying on the bed, with one hand shackled to the bedpost. The image made her stomach tighten again, but she held onto it.

"Trevor," she called softly. "Trevor, it's Mommy. I've come back to talk to you again—like we did last night."

Her breathing shallow, she waited for some response, trying to reach out to her son with her mind, but she couldn't make anything happen. Well, she could imagine a conversation, but she knew it was only something she was making up. Which reinforced the conviction that the previous contact had been the real thing.

When she realized her muscles were tied in knots, she forced herself to relax and do some of the deep-breathing exercises that she'd learned in a yoga class. She succeeded in dispelling some of her tension, but she simply couldn't locate Trevor. It was as though she'd had a television cable hookup last night with the Trevor channel. This morning, it wasn't in the lineup.

That thought sent a wave of panic crashing over her. What if the man called Blue had killed him?

No! She wouldn't let that be true, and it didn't make sense. Why would they go to all this trouble to activate Trevor's I gene if they were just going to kill him?

But what if it had happened anyway? What if they'd given him too much of the treatment too fast—and it had killed him? Or knocked him unconscious?

Unable to stand the thoughts churning in her head, she jumped out of bed and stood staring out the window—her vision blurred by a sheen of tears.

That was how Matt found her when he came back with a cardboard tray filled with coffee, muffins and hard-boiled eggs.

As soon as he saw her, he set the tray down on the table and reached for her.

"What is it? Did you talk to him? Did he tell you something bad?"

It took an effort, but she managed not to start sobbing. "No. It's just the opposite. I couldn't get through to him at all, and I started imagining all kinds of horrible things."

He stroked her back and hair. "Don't do that to yourself."

"Why couldn't I talk to him the way I could last night?"

"There are a lot of reasons. It could be simple—like he's sleeping."

"He reached me in my sleep."

"Maybe it doesn't work the other way. Or maybe it's because he's just learning to use his ability. It's not reliable. Or it's still new, and it comes and goes."

She nodded against his shoulder. "Or he's with Blue right now, and he's afraid that he'll give himself away if he tries it."

"Right. That's another possibility."

When she caught a strained look on his face, she asked, "What are you thinking now?"

"Nothing."

"Tell me!"

"I was thinking that there may be a limit to how far Trevor can project. If Blue moved him farther away, maybe he can't reach you anymore."

She couldn't hold back a little cry. "No!"

"I'm sorry, it popped into my head."

"But you could be right. I mean, they could even take him out of the country."

"That's kind of risky for them, don't you think?"

She fisted her hands in frustration. "I'm getting hyper again."

"You're his mother. Of course you're upset, but let's try to get back to something normal. Do you want to get dressed or eat first?"

She looked at the food he'd brought without enthusiasm. "It doesn't matter."

"Then get dressed. That may make you feel more in control."

When she came out of the bathroom wearing jeans and a shirt, Matt had made the bed and was sitting with his back propped against the pillows watching TV.

"Anything we should watch out for?"

"The parking-lot shooting incident made the local news."

"Do they have any more information than we did?"

"They're looking for the couple who were staying in room twenty-three."

"Oh, great."

"They have a sort of description of me. Height and weight. Hair color. They didn't see you."

"What are you going to do?"

"Shave my head?"

"The Bruce Willis look?"

"Yeah."

She sat down on the other side of the bed where he'd placed her coffee cup, muffin and egg. The coffee was cold, but it didn't really matter.

And the muffin tasted like cardboard. After eating about a third of it, she said, "I've been trying to come up with another angle, but I guess we'd better call the FBI."

"Okay. Jack gave me a number for the task force that's working on the case."

When he pulled a slip of paper out of his shirt pocket, she knew he'd come prepared.

IN THE PARKING LOT of the motel, two other people were having a quick breakfast—Bobby Savage and Don Campbell. The man they were working for had told them Whitlock and Young were on a mission, a mission they must not be allowed to complete. Because Bobby knew he had to find them and stop them, desperation had kept him and Don up all night, checking every motel in or near Rapid City. They'd finally gotten lucky—just when they'd almost decided to give up and beat a retreat to somewhere like Vancouver.

A clerk who was going off duty remembered a guy checking in late at night. A guy who looked like he was running from the law, the clerk said. And when Bobby showed him the picture he'd been given, the clerk said it was him.

Which meant they were back in business and waiting for Whitlock and Young to come out so they could scoop them up.

Don craned his neck toward the door. "Nothing yet."

"Maybe they're sleeping in. They had a rough night."

"So did we."

"What do you think they're doing here?" Bobby asked.

"Maybe they're looking for money from a big heist."

"Yeah, that makes sense."

"You think we could grab the loot and split?"

"Let's play that by ear."

They didn't say what they were both thinking. Losing the couple hadn't been their fault. That damn GPS thing had stopped working, but they were the ones who were going to catch heat for the slip-up. Which meant that they'd better get it right this time.

SHELLEY LOOKED at the phone number Jack had provided. "Is that in Washington, D.C.?"

"I don't know."

"Is it better to call from a cell phone or from this motel?"

He thought about that for a few minutes. "You mean, which is easier to trace?"

"Yes."

He shrugged. They can probably figure out where the call is coming from either way. But if we use the motel phone, we can leave right away, assuming they don't have somebody in town ready to swoop down on us."

"You think they could?"

"No, I was just trying to give you the worst case."

"Let's go with the best case—that they know where to find Trevor."

"Right. Do you want to listen in on the call from the extension?"

"Yes."

"Okay. But let me do the talking."

"You think I'll break down?" she asked in a tight voice.

"No. But I think it's less confusing if only one person speaks."

She nodded and went into the other room, where she found that the second phone was a portable. Hurrying back to the doorway, she held it up to show Matt.

"Okay. Good."

The phone beside the bed was a conventional landline. After picking up the receiver, he dialed and waited.

The woman who answered said, "FBI field office. How may I direct your call?"

As she listened on the other line, the question made Shelley realize that they should have talked about their approach. What was Matt going to say now?

He glanced at Shelley, then said, "I'm calling in regard to an operation involving a place called the Facility."

"One moment please."

He was put on hold—complete with light classical music playing over the line. Was the delay so the FBI could trace the call?

Still clutching the extension phone, Shelley walked to the chair in the corner and sat down. Matt took his cue from her and sat on the bed.

After about a minute, a man came on the line.

"This is special agent Perry Owens. How can I help you?"

"We're trying to locate our missing son."

"To whom am I speaking?"

"I'd rather not say over the phone," Matt answered.

"Where did you get this number?"

Matt sighed, and she knew he was starting to realize that he wasn't going to get very far into the conversation unless he established that he had a legitimate reason for calling.

"Jack Maddox told me you might be able to help."

"You're the man and woman who visited him yesterday?"

Shelley struggled to hold back a gasp.

"How do you know that?" Matt demanded.

The guy didn't beat around the bush. "We have his house under surveillance."

Shelley was starting to feel that they'd stepped into an episode of *The Twilight Zone*. "Okay. Yes, that was us."

"Matt Whitlock and Shelley Young."

"Yes," Matt growled.

"Did you get into some trouble in Rapid City last night?"

"Yes," he admitted.

"What happened, exactly?"

"I guess we should wait on that till we get there."

"Agreed," the guy on the other end of the line said in a dry voice.

Just from this brief conversation, Shelley didn't like Perry Owens, but making value judgments over the phone wasn't going to do Trevor any good. Apparently Matt concurred because he said, "We'd appreciate any help you can give us to find our son."

"We've taken over the Facility. Why don't you come here and we can talk about your problem?"

"How do we get there?"

"I recommend that you don't take a direct route."

"All right."

The man gave Matt directions. "We'll be expecting you in the next couple of hours."

"All right."

He hung up and looked at Shelley.

"That didn't sound too friendly," she commented, after hanging up her own phone.

"Yeah."

"He knows we visited Jack Maddox. He knows our names. He knows we got into some trouble last night. In other words—they've been keeping track of *us*."

"I think it's because they have Jack's place under surveillance. Once we visited him, we got onto their radar."

"Is that good or bad?"

"I don't know yet. I guess we'll find out when we get to the Facility. Too bad they didn't send help when those guys were after us."

"How did they get our names?" Shelley asked.

"They could have gotten mine from the license number of the rental car. Then they worked their way back to you."

"Charming. Did we make a mistake?"

"With everything they know about us, I don't think it makes any difference."

She nodded.

"We'll pack up and get on the road."

They hadn't taken much out of their luggage, so it was easy to get ready.

When Matt had set their bags next to the door, he looked out the window, checking the parking lot. "I don't see anyone, but we'd better not take any chances."

"Who are we looking for? The bad guys—or the law?" she asked.

"Either or both." He was silent for a moment. "I'll take the bags down and check out. Then I'll pull up at the entrance near this room. When you see the car, come down and get in."

"Okay."

He hesitated for a moment, then gathered her into his embrace and folded her close. Her arms came around him, holding tight, and they clung together for a long moment. "I'm sorry," she murmured.

"For what?"

"Getting you into all this trouble."

"You didn't have a choice. Neither did I."

"I could have gone straight to the FBI and skipped all the chasing around."

"You would have been terrified to do that."

"I'm still terrified."

"We both are."

"You handle it pretty well."

"I'm glad it looks that way."

He hugged her more tightly, and she rested her head on his shoulder, thankful that she wasn't in this alone. She'd been afraid to find out how he'd react to the news that he had a child, but he'd immediately offered to help her find their son. Now he was into the search as deeply as she was.

"We'd better get the show on the road," he finally said as he eased away. "I wish I could call you on your cell phone."

"Too bad the battery gave out before I got to your house."

"Yeah. You'll have to watch at the window. Then come down as soon as I pull up with the car."

After he'd left the room, she walked to the window, knowing that it would take a little time for him to check out. Also knowing there was a lot that could go wrong in the next few minutes.

Time dragged as she waited for the rental car to appear below the window.

When she finally saw Matt, she let out the breath she'd been holding. But just as he slowed down, another car fell in line behind him.

Instead of pulling up at the curb, he shot away, and she saw him pick up speed as he roared out of the parking lot, then onto the highway.

SHELLEY'S HEART leaped into her throat as she watched Matt vanish, with the other car in hot pursuit.

Oh, Lord, it must be the men from last night. Somehow they'd found Matt. What was he going to do? Could he get away from them? Or would they catch him?

And what was *she* going to do? Matt had reminded her that she couldn't use her cell phone. How was she going to hook up with him again?

Although the two cars had disappeared, she stayed at the window, searching the distance and the parking lot. But neither of the vehicles reappeared, which gave her only temporary safety. If the men didn't find Matt, they might come back here looking for her. She couldn't stay in this room.

Or in the motel?

Matt had stowed their luggage in the car. She had only her purse with her. After taking one more look out the window, she crossed to the sitting area then stepped into the hall. When she closed the door behind her, she realized she couldn't get back inside because Matt had taken the only key. And he'd checked out, anyway.

She hurried down the stairs and out into the frigid morning air, thinking that she was up the creek without a paddle.

Matt had the number of the FBI. He also had Jack's number, which she could get from the Web, she supposed, if she had access to a computer.

Struggling against the trapped feeling compressing her chest, she headed back into the lobby, but she couldn't just wait where anyone who came in could see her. Matt had come down here for breakfast. Was that room still open?

MATT SHOT DOWN the road, scrambling for a way to thwart the guys following him. Last night they'd passed a section of town that was crawling with fast-food restaurants. That meant tons of parking lots with people getting in and out of cars. A good place to lose the tail.

He turned in at a well-known chain with a playground out in front, craning his neck as he passed the drive-through. There was only one lane, so he couldn't get around the building that way.

With the bad guys close behind him, he plowed through the parking lot, barely missing a man and woman coming out with bags of food.

They jumped back onto the curb as he and the other car roared past.

What were the odds of getting away? Could he use his talent to send the other car in the wrong direction?

He tried giving the driver behind him a silent message, but the other vehicle stayed with him, and he assumed that the car chase was interfering with his concentration.

After rounding a pile of snow between two parking areas, he whipped around another building.

This one had a wider drive-through lane and he turned in there, listening to horns honk as people assumed he was trying to cut in line.

Glancing in the rearview mirror, he saw the driver of a pickup truck pull out, presumably with his order, cutting off the car pursuing Matt. He took the opportunity to plunge into the next parking lot, then around another building.

When he looked behind him, he saw that he'd lost the pursuers. Was it safe to take the highway back to the motel? Or did he need to keep up this game of hide and seek for a while longer?

As his thoughts turned to Shelley, his throat clogged. She'd been looking for him out the window, and she must have seen him drive away with the other car right behind him. She had to be terrified.

Dammit, she didn't even have a phone. Well, when they hooked up again, he'd remedy that.

If they hooked up again. No, cancel that. He was going to go back there and get her.

WALKING SWIFTLY past the front desk, Shelley followed the signs to the room where breakfast had been served.

A blond woman in a maid's uniform shook her head. "I'm sorry, honey. We closed a half hour ago, but you can get coffee down by the pool."

"Thank you," she answered and kept walking, down the hall toward the weight room and indoor pool.

After stepping into the exercise area, she opened the door a crack and looked back. The maid was still standing there, so she made a circuit of the room, inspecting the various machines. It wasn't bad for a motel facility. When she opened the door to the pool area, a blast of heated, chlorine-scented air hit her, and she dodged back.

How long would she have to wait for Matt? And what should she do if he didn't come back?

If she called the FBI in Washington, would they admit that they had agents stationed at the Facility? Maybe if she told them she'd spoken to Perry Owens? Unfortunately, he wouldn't confirm that, because she'd stayed silent on the phone while Matt had done the talking.

Feeling as though she was wandering through the hedgerows of a maze with no exit, she walked back down the hall toward the breakfast room. When she didn't see the maid who had warned her away, she turned the door knob.

The door wasn't locked, and she was able to slip inside. After her eyes adjusted to the dim light, she inspected her surroundings. The room was about thirty feet long and fifteen feet wide with about twenty tables—some for two and some for four.

Along one wall was a serving counter that was mostly empty except for stacks of trays. Beside the counter was a refrigerator case and at the end of the counter was another door. Hoping to find a closet where she could hide or another exit, she pulled the door open and found a storage area lined with shelves for paper goods and other supplies.

The only way out of here was where she'd come in. Unless she could get a window open.

When she tried one, she found it was fixed in place with no opening mechanism.

And this room wasn't at the front of the building, so she wouldn't be able to see Matt drive up if he was able to come back for her.

She struggled to stay calm as she considered her options.

She could call the local police, but then she might end up in jail for disturbing the peace, since there was only her word for it that she and Matt hadn't been the ones shooting up the parking lot at the other motel. And was shooting a gun in a populated area more serious than just disturbing the peace?

Her mind continued to spin. Could she get to the Facility on her own? She'd listened to Owens giving them directions, but she hadn't written them down. And probably she wasn't going to be able to take a cab there.

She ground her teeth. Every alternative she thought of ended in a blank wall—or disaster.

Pulling the blinds aside so she'd have a little light, she dug into her purse to find her wallet.

How much cash did she have?

Not much more than a hundred dollars, which wasn't going to get her very far. And Matt hadn't used an ATM, which meant she shouldn't do that, either.

DON CAMPBELL slapped the steering wheel with his palms. "You see if you can scoop her up. I'll go back to the fast-food joints."

"I don't like splitting up."

"You got a better idea?"

"No," Bobby Savage answered as he climbed out of the car and turned toward the main entrance of the hotel. He took a deep breath and let it out before walking into the lobby. The clerk who'd been on duty here last night had been cooperative. But there was another guy on the desk this morning. Would he give out information about guests?

And which was the best approach to take? Pretending to be a cop or pretending to be a friend of Whitlock and Young?

He'd make that decision when he walked up to the desk and got a closer look at the clerk.

SHELLEY FELT like a mouse huddled in a hole. Or was it more like being a sitting duck?

What if she left the breakfast room? Could she tell one of the staff that she was waiting for Matt?

They'd probably direct her to the bar, which was more exposed than she was now.

Out in the lobby, she heard someone speaking in a loud voice.

Quietly she tiptoed across the room and eased the door open. A man was standing at the front desk, talking with the clerk.

She froze as she realized he was one of the men she'd seen last night.

Chapter Nine

"Certainly you can look around, detective," the clerk said.

Before he could turn, Shelley eased the door closed and looked wildly around the darkened breakfast area for something to use as a weapon and somewhere to hide. The best she could do was race to other side of the room, grab some of the metal trays from the counter and duck down behind one of the tables.

Seconds after she'd lowered herself to the floor, someone yanked open the door.

She couldn't be sure it was the man who was pretending to be a detective, but that was an excellent guess.

As she waited with her heart pounding, she prayed that he would go away. Instead he turned on the light and took several steps into the room.

Slowly he began to walk around the tables, his footsteps coming closer and closer.

With the light on, her hiding place didn't give her much shelter, and she wasn't surprised to hear a gruff voice say,

"Get up."

"Who are you?"

"I said, get up."

She knew that if he got his hands on her, there would be no one to save her son, but as he moved rapidly toward her, she saw that he had a gun in his hand, and that changed everything.

She'd thought she could throw the trays at him, Frisbee style, and get out of the room. That wasn't such a hot idea when he was pointing a weapon at her.

Could she throw the tray across the floor so he'd think there was someone else in here? Or what if she pretended to faint from fear? He'd have to bend down, and then she could whack his gun hand with the tray.

She was desperate enough to try it. Before she could act, the door burst open again and another figure barreled inside.

It was Matt.

When he heard the door, the man turned quickly. But Shelley was just as quick.

She threw the tray with a flick of her wrist, catching the man in the back of the neck with the edge. He cried out as he went down.

"Watch out, he's got a pistol," she shouted.

Matt leaped on the gunman, trying to grab the weapon, but the thug had recovered from the blow to his neck and started wrestling with Matt.

Her heart wedged into her throat as they rolled across the floor, grunting and growling as each of them struggled for control of the weapon.

With her gaze fixed on them, she wove through the tables, raising the tray above her head, trying to time her assault on the bad guy.

When the assailant rolled on top of Matt, she held the tray so that the edge was facing downward, them rammed it onto the top of the thug's head.

He went still, and Matt grabbed the gun, shoving it into his coat pocket before scrambling up.

"Come on."

They were almost to the door when the manager and the desk clerk charged into the room.

"What's going on?" the manager demanded.

"Call the police," Matt shouted. "That man attacked us."

"He said he was a detective," the desk clerk answered.

"He's lying," Matt shot back.

As the staffers started toward the guy on the floor, Matt grabbed Shelley's hand.

He led her out of the room, through the door, and to the car, which he'd pulled up under the marquee at the front entrance. Opening the door, he practically shoved her inside, then sprinted around to the driver's side and got in.

The desk clerk was running toward them now.

"Stop. You have to wait for the police."

Matt didn't bother answering as he sped away from the building.

In the distance she could hear a police siren. But they were out of the parking lot before they spotted a patrol car.

She watched out the back window for several minutes, making sure they weren't being followed, then turned in her seat, surprised at the view. They'd left the urban area behind, and all around them were pine forests and mountains, with big rock formations rising out of the trees.

"Are you okay?" Matt asked.

"Yes."

"I'm sorry I had to leave you."

"You didn't have a choice. I saw that car pull up behind you. How did you get away from them?"

"There's a whole bunch of fast-food restaurants down the street from the motel. I headed there and zipped in and out of parking lots, dodging pedestrians. Probably the other guy's still there, looking for me."

"How did you know where to find me?"

"The maid. She saw you go into the breakfast room after he'd told you it was closed, and she was getting ready to inform the manager."

"I thought I'd given her the slip. I guess she was still keeping tabs on me."

Matt turned left onto a two-lane highway. "I was terrified I wasn't going to find you," he said in a rough voice.

"I didn't know what to do after you left."

"You did the right thing, staying at the motel."

"Except that the guy came back looking for me."

"I'm sorry."

"Not your fault."

"I should have been more careful when I went outside. But they were parked between two cars in the lot, and I didn't see them until it was too late."

"How did they find us?"

"I guess they were asking around—and somebody gave them a tip. Maybe the clerk who checked us in."

"Will they come after us again?"

"I hope not," Matt said, but she could tell by his tone that they shouldn't count on being in the clear.

MATT REACHED for her hand and gripped it tightly. Now that they were out of danger, Shelley had started to shake, and frankly he wasn't doing much better.

He'd been scared spitless when he'd started thinking about how she would react to the unexpected change in plans. It was a miracle that they were back in the car together. Or maybe it was a sign that their luck had changed.

Pulling off the road onto the shoulder, he reached for her across the console and gathered her into his arms, hugging her tightly.

"It's okay," he murmured, reassuring himself as well as her. "Everything's going to be okay."

She closed her eyes and leaned into him, and they clung together for long moments.

"I don't want that to happen again. We need phones," she said when she finally spoke.

"We won't get separated again. And we don't have time to stop now. We're already late."

She closed her eyes, hanging on to him fiercely. "That was awful."

"I know. It was awful for me, too," he admitted in a gritty voice. "I kept worrying about where you were going to be. And worrying about what I was going to do if I couldn't find you." He stroked her arm. "Then I charged into the breakfast room and that goon had gotten there first. Are you okay?"

"As okay as I can be. Under the circumstances."

"Yeah. I guess I mean—are you ready to go to the Facility?"

"That was the plan."

He looked at the directions the FBI agent had given him, then pulled back out onto the highway. "Watch for a small sign at a crossroads that says 250," he said. "It will be on the right."

She kept her gaze trained to the right of the shoulder and pointed to the sign after a couple of miles.

"There."

He turned onto a gravel road that had been kept plowed. It was wide enough for only one vehicle at a time. Looming ahead of them was a mountain rising out of the forest.

When they came to a chain-link fence with a gatehouse, he slowed. A man in heavy coat, knit cap and jeans tucked into high boots met them as they came to a stop.

"What's your business here?"

"Matt Whitlock and Shelley Young to see Special Agent Owens."

"Can I see some identification please?"

They both fished their drivers' licenses out of their wallets and handed them to the guard who looked at them for several moments before handing them back.

"Would you open the trunk?"

Matt sprang the latch, and the guard ducked his head under the door, presumably looking through their luggage.

When he returned to the guardhouse, he picked up a telephone and pressed a sequence of numbers. After a brief conversation, he opened the automatic gate.

"I guess they don't want anyone wandering in here," Shelley murmured.

"Apparently."

As Matt drove through and continued along the road leading toward the mountain, his heart was pounding. He had to assume that he'd been here before. For three months. But none of it looked familiar.

The road ended in a larger, plowed gravel area where several cars were parked. Beyond it was a door built into what looked like solid rock.

"Fortress America," Shelley whispered.

"Yeah. And you can bet that every inch of the way from the time we drove through the gate is under video surveillance."

She nodded in the direction they'd come. "And probably cameras in the trees leading up to the gate, too."

They climbed out of the car and approached the door. Before they reached it, a man stepped out.

Since he wasn't dressed for the South Dakota winter, they followed him quickly inside.

When the door shut automatically behind them, Matt had to fight a trapped sensation.

He'd been held here against his will, but this was different, he told himself. Crazy scientists had been running the place back then. Now the FBI was in charge.

"Special Agent Perry Owens," the man said, holding out his hand.

"Matt Whitlock."

"And Shelley Young."

Each of them shook hands with the agent.

As they followed him through another door, Matt sized him up. He was a big man, six feet tall and well muscled, with prematurely gray hair. Even out here in the middle of nowhere, he was dressed in a crisp white shirt, suit and tie.

"This is a natural cave," he said. "It was a Cold War secure facility."

"A fallout shelter?" Matt asked, struggling to hold his voice steady. He'd known that coming back here would affect him, but he hadn't wanted to admit—even to himself—how bad it would be.

"Yeah. But then it was decommissioned, and the government lost track of it. How much do you know about what went on here?"

Matt related what Jack and Claudia had told them. As Matt spoke, Owens kept his gaze fixed on him. "And you were one of the test subjects?"

"Yes," Matt admitted.

"You were taken when you were twelve?"

"Yeah. You know an awful lot about me."

"We have some of Sykes's records. Your case is one of the ones that appeared in the files."

He forced himself to keep silent. He was here to get information, not to reveal how much this place was spooking him.

"Would you like a tour?" Owens asked, and Matt struggled to hear him over the ringing in his ears.

"We're hoping you can help us find our son," Shelley broke in.

"Yes. Trevor." Owens looked from one of them to the other. "Your son was born after the two of you broke up." He turned to Matt. "And you didn't know about the boy until Ms. Young came to you a couple of days ago."

"That's right," Matt snapped.

"How did you feel about that?"

"I was shocked at first. Then I knew I would do everything in my power to help Shelley find Trevor."

"That's very noble of you."

"Noble?" That was an odd way to put it. "Are you a parent?" Matt asked, still fighting to keep his voice even.

"No, I'm not."

"Then you wouldn't understand."

"Mmm. I'd like to show you around," Owens said, firmly changing the subject. Apparently it was okay to pry into Matt and Shelley's personal lives, but not into the agent's.

Their footsteps echoed hollowly in the dimly lit corridors as Owens led them further into the mountain.

The perfect prison, Matt thought. No windows, and only one exit that was easily guarded.

He wished he could use his talent on this guy to pry some information out of him, but he suspected Owens would be ready for that. If he'd read Matt's file, he would know what to guard against.

They came to a place where water seeped through a crack in the ceiling, leaving a stain down the wall and on the floor. Had it been in disrepair when Sykes had used it? Or was it not being maintained now?

"These rooms are where the staff slept," Owens said, leading them down a side corridor with more doors on either side. Matt opened a door and saw a room that wasn't much more appealing than the cell that he remembered. It had a narrow bed, a dresser and a closet. At the end of the hallway was a lounge furnished with stiff-looking sofas and chairs.

"Not very comfortable," Shelley murmured.

Owens didn't comment.

"Is this a hardship assignment?" she asked.

He shrugged.

They retraced their steps, then went on to new territory. Owens showed them the laboratories, which had been full of equipment when Matt had been there. Now the rooms were empty. Still, he could remember the old setup with a clarity he wished he could dull.

The next stop was the cell block. When he saw the small rooms with metal doors and viewing windows, he fought a wave of nausea.

Shelley moved beside him and took his arm. "You remember this?" she murmured.

"Yeah." To prove to himself that he could do it, he pulled open one of the doors and stepped into the tiny cell. When he'd been here before, the room had been brightly lit, but the lights were dimmed now, probably to conserve energy.

He looked around at the bunk, the toilet, the sink. Almost like a prison.

Fighting a feeling of claustrophobia, he stepped into the hall and took a deep breath of the dank air.

He wanted to ask if all of the subjects had survived the experiments, but he knew that if Owens gave him the wrong answer, it would be devastating to Shelley. Instead he asked, "How many subjects did Sykes work on?"

"At least fifty that we know about."

"Over what period?"

"More than twenty years."

Matt nodded. He wanted to get out of here, but he couldn't cut the visit short until they got what they were here for—information about Trevor.

"If this place is so well guarded, how did I get away?" he asked.

Owens stopped walking and turned to him. "That's one of the interesting things in the files. As you know, Sykes discovered that the younger an individual, the better the result when they activated the I gene."

"Yeah."

Owens continued in a flat voice. "After the enhancing treatment, he released certain subjects so they could go back into the world and breed—thus providing him with a fresh group of youngsters to work with."

As the words penetrated Matt's brain, he stumbled and would have fallen if he hadn't caught himself with a hand against the wall.

"Excuse me?" he said.

"You were released as a breeder. Sykes wanted you to have children, so he could experiment on them."

Shelley gasped. "But it's a recessive gene. He'd need a mother who also carried the I gene."

"True. I believe he had various ways of checking the general population. In college, did you participate in any blood drives?"

"Yes," she answered.

"Sykes arranged for several colleges and universities to test for the I gene during student blood drives."

Her face had hardened. "That's...unethical."

"The whole experiment was unethical. That never dissuaded him. He had a series of experiments he wanted to perform, and he was going to carry them out, no matter what the cost to any individual." Owens gave her a speculative look. "You went to work for Matt as an accountant after you graduated from college. How did you happen to meet him?"

"Through the college job center. I went there at the end of my senior year, looking for suitable employment." Her gaze turned inward. "The man who interviewed me encouraged me to apply for a position at Matt's ranch." She sucked in a sharp breath and let it out. "Are you saying the college job center was in on the...conspiracy?"

"It would seem so. Or they had someone from the project working in the office. If he got an applicant with the I gene, he matched them up with someone else who had the gene. If he could, of course."

Matt couldn't hold back a curse. He'd known that he'd been used for unethical purposes; he hadn't known Shelley had also been manipulated into getting together with him—so they could produce a child who would fit the specifications for the project.

"After you left the ranch, they obviously kept tabs on you," Owen added helpfully.

"Wait a minute," Matt growled. "Let me get this straight. If Sykes is no longer working for the government, who's funding him?"

"As far as we can tell, a group called the Association."

"And who the hell are they?" Matt snapped.

"They're made up of representatives from several foreign governments who are interested in his enhancement techniques. We know that much, but not who they are because they are determined to protect their identities at all costs. They want the benefits of Sykes research, and they're willing to pay for it, but they're not willing to have anyone know they're funding him."

Matt spent a few seconds processing that information; as he did, a horrible truth began to form in his mind. Looking Owens directly in the eye, he asked, "I suppose you have no idea where to find Sykes?"

"Correct."

He glanced at Shelley, whose face had taken on a queasy look. He hated to hurt her further, but he had to clarify something else. "Also, you don't have any idea where Trevor is being held? Or by whom?"

At least the man had the grace to appear uncomfortable. "I'm afraid not. After we closed this place down, the doctor decided it was safer not to have one central lab. He's using facilities that are at a number of different locations."

Again, Matt considered the information—and the source. "So you asked us to come here, and you've just been touring us around this place purely to get my reactions."

Owens spread his hands. "It's important that we obtain as much information as possible. Any clue we can get from you could make it easier for us to find Sykes."

"Thanks a lot."

"The more we know, the more likely we'll be able to come up with the doctor's present whereabouts."

If he stayed here much longer he was going to strangle the FBI agent. Taking Shelley's arm, Matt started back the way they'd come.

Before they'd gotten very far, Owens called out, "Wait a minute."

Matt stopped and turned. "Why should we?"

"There's one more thing I want to show you."

He was torn. The guy was cold-bloodedly using them to get information for the U.S. government, and Matt had the suspicion that he wasn't going to like this "one more thing." But maybe there was some way to turn the tables on the agent.

Matt turned to Shelley, hating the devastated look on her face. "Are you willing to stay for a few more minutes?"

She considered the question, then answered in a barely audible voice, "Yes."

Their footsteps echoed hollowly in the empty corridors as Owens led them down another darkened hallway, this time to a part of the Facility near the labs.

They walked into a room where the temperature was low and the walls were lined with stainless-steel drawers.

Matt had a sense of what was coming and put his arm around Shelley, as Owens pulled one of the drawers open. Inside was the naked body of a woman. It took a moment for Matt to understand what he was seeing as he stared at the terrible wound in her midsection.

"She was pregnant?" he asked in a harsh voice.

"It seems so."

"And the baby is missing."

Beside him, Shelley made a high-pitched sound. He felt her waver on her feet and caught her in his arms.

Her head lolled back, and her face was white as paste.

"You bastard," he said to Owens as he carried her outside.

They had passed a room along the hall with several chairs. Matt strode inside, cradling Shelley on his lap, stroking her hair as he spoke softly to her.

She had fainted, but she was coming around by the time he sat down.

Her eyes blinked open and she stared at him, horror written across her face.

"Was that real?" she asked.

Matt looked at Owens. "Was it? Or just another sideshow for our reaction."

"I believe it was what it looked like."

"That poor woman. Who is she?" Shelley asked.

"I was hoping you could tell us."

"Like you think it's my mother or something?" Matt shot back.

"We know it's not your mother. But it might be someone you've seen before."

"No."

He held Shelley in his arms and leaned his head back against the wall, struggling for calm. His memories of this place were bad, but they had been limited to his own experiences in one cell and the medical facility. Now he knew that all kinds of atrocities had gone on in this house of horrors. Things he couldn't have imagined in a million years. No wonder they called it "the Facility." They didn't want the name to convey any of the real purpose.

Shelley stirred in his arms. "This is like Nazi Germany," she whispered.

"Yeah. I was thinking something like that," Matt answered.

Owens shook his head. "Nazi Germany's policies were

widely known by the population. What went on in this lab when it was operational was mostly hidden from even government sources."

"But somebody in the government knew about it."

"We shut it down when we found out. And we're trying to find Dr. Sykes right now. Do you understand the urgency of that mission?"

"Yes," Shelley answered. "But it doesn't do us any good."

"I'm sorry."

As Matt listened, a plan began to form in his mind. In a decisive voice, he said, "You are going to help us."

Owens looked at him. "We have only so much manpower, and our big push is to identify the members of the Association. I'm afraid we can't allocate any resources to any of the individual victims."

"I understand that, but I have some additional information that you'll find useful."

"Like what?"

"I'll tell you in exchange for your help."

Chapter Ten

Matt watched Owens's face, waiting with his pulse pounding. This guy had lured a couple of desperate parents to the Facility to serve his own agenda. Now he was calculating the pros and cons of doing something for them—if it suited his purposes.

"What else do you know?" the agent asked.

"I'd like something from you, first. Since you know there are two guys following us around, do us a favor and get them off our backs. Because if they stop us, we're not going to find our son. Plus, if you capture them, you'll find out who they're working for. Probably it's Sykes, and you can flush him out."

The agent considered the suggestions. "This would be a limited arrangement," he said.

"Yes."

"What do you have in mind?"

"Shelley and I will go back to town. We'll drive around so the bad guys can spot us. Then we'll check into another motel and wait for them to pounce. Only this time, you'll be covering us—ready to bag them before they can do anything serious."

"You're putting yourselves in danger."

"We're willing to take that chance," Matt said, then glanced at Shelley for confirmation.

She answered with a little nod, and he wondered how much she liked the plan. After her personal contact with one of the thugs, she must not be looking forward to more, but she wasn't saying no.

They all walked down the hall to an office full of computers and communications equipment. It wasn't fancy, but it was certainly well-equipped.

"Have a seat," Owens said. "We need to bring agent Parker in on this to evaluate what you have for us."

They took seats across from a desk, while Owens went to get the other agent.

Shelley made a small sound when they were alone. "Do you really have something more for them?"

"Oh yeah."

"You're not going to tell the…"

He pressed his finger to her lips, then said in a low voice. "They're probably listening to us."

"Oh. Right."

Owens was gone for several minutes—probably waiting to see if they'd say anything good while he was out of the room.

When he returned, he introduced them to a short, heavyset man who looked more like a Mafia wise guy than an FBI agent.

"I hear you people want to play sitting ducks," the man said in a conversational voice.

"If you want to call it that," Matt answered. "Let's make sure nothing bad happens."

They discussed various strategies. When they'd agreed on a plan, Parker said, "What's the information you have for us?"

"The men were able to follow us around because I had a transponder under my skin. They tracked us to one motel—then another."

Owens stared at him. "And they're tracking you here, too?"

"I found it and took it out."

"Found it how?"

"Logical deduction. I figured they couldn't have tagged my rental car, so it had to be me."

"Where is it?"

"Flushed down a motel toilet."

"So you say."

"It was in my groin area."

"Let's see."

Matt gave him a hard look then stood up and unbuckled his belt. After unzipping his pants, he dropped them to the bandage on his inner thigh.

"It was there."

"Interesting location," Owens observed dryly.

"Yeah. Maybe other people in the project have them, too. That might be useful to you."

Both agents nodded.

Matt looked at Shelley. "Let's get the show on the road."

"One more thing," Parker said. "If you find your son, we want to interview him,"

"We'll think about it."

"It's part of the deal," Owens shot back.

"All right," Matt agreed, then glanced at Shelley, who gave a little nod.

Parker handed Shelley a small metal disk. "Put this in your purse, and we'll be able to track you—like with that transponder in Matt. Only this one's external."

"Okay."

"You won't see us. But we'll be waiting for your shadows to close in."

They nailed down a few more details, then Matt and Shelley left the underground facility.

As they stepped into the sunlight, Matt took a deep breath of the forest air.

"That place smells like mold," he said.

"It smells like evil."

"That, too. And not just from the past. I get the feeling those agents are as ruthless as Sykes."

"But you're willing to work with them."

"If I have to."

She gave him a long look. "Are you really going to let them question Trevor?"

"I'm sure that was in their plans all along, but I'm not going to let them bother him right away. I'm going to insist on some time alone—just the three of us," he said, feeling his chest tighten as he spoke.

Her next question was, "Do you trust Owens?"

"Not entirely. But I think he's decided that my proposition is to his advantage. So he'll go along with us. And if by *trust* you mean do I think he'd let those guys grab us, no, I don't."

"I guess that's right. Unless he's working with them."

Matt's head swung toward her. "Are you serious?"

"I don't know what to think." She dragged in a breath. "In the grand scheme of things, I don't believe those agents are all that concerned about one little boy, but I'm guessing that this case could be an embarrassment to the U.S. government."

"If it got out."

"If we don't get our son back, I'll make sure it does," she said in a steely voice.

Matt was thinking they could disappear just as easily as Trevor, but he kept the observation to himself.

As they approached the gate, Matt found he was holding his breath while he waited for the guard to let them out.

When they'd cleared the enclosure, Shelley turned her head back to look at the mountain rising out of the pine forest. "That place is in such a beautiful location. The forest setting, and the rock formations are majestic. But then you get inside, and you realize the Facility is straight out of a nightmare."

"Yeah."

"Every time I think about your being there as a little boy, I want to scream—or cry."

"I thought I'd escaped on my own. Apparently they wanted to let me go free—so I could provide them with more test subjects."

"I'm glad you got out," she whispered. "And don't tell me you put me and Trevor in danger. Like I said, it's not just you. I'm as much involved." She sighed.

"What?"

"My parents were still alive when I graduated from college. I remember how they urged me to visit the school job center. Do you think someone planted the idea in their minds?"

"Knowing what we do now, I can believe it."

They were both silent for several moments, then he heard her make a small sound. "What?"

"The image of that poor woman in the freezer keeps popping into my mind."

"Yeah. But don't get hung up on her."

"It's hard not to. I think about carrying Trevor—and having somebody cut him out of me before he was born."

He swore. "Don't do that to yourself."

"I'm trying not to."

She leaned back and closed her eyes, and for a few minutes, she looked as though she might be going to sleep. Then she sat up straighter and said, "Trevor?"

Matt's head swung toward her. "You heard him again?"

"Yes. Just for a minute. Then he was gone again."

"But that tells us he's okay."

She turned toward him. "What if we started driving, and I tried seeing if I could pick up his voice more strongly—or less?"

"You think we can find him that way?"

"Yes!"

He wasn't so sure, but he wasn't going to argue the point because it gave Shelley hope. And she needed that after what they'd both seen in the Facility.

"We'll try it," he agreed, "But I think we need to go through with the current plans first, because those guys following us have a bad habit of catching up. I'd like to neutralize them before we do anything else."

She nodded. "Okay."

He watched the tense set of her mouth. "I'm guessing you want to go after Trevor now."

"Yes, but I understand why it's better to finish with the FBI deal first. Not just to get those thugs off our backs—we made an agreement with Owens and Parker, and if we don't go through with it, they aren't going to help us again if we need them."

"Right."

They circled around, taking roads through the pine forests and the rock outcroppings, making sure nobody could figure out where they'd been before they headed back to town.

The first thing Matt did was stop at an electronics store where he bought Shelley a cell phone and had it activated. Then they started looking for a suitable motel.

They'd discussed the location with Owens and concluded that a tourist site with cabins was the best choice, because that allowed the bad guys to sneak up on them and also gave the FBI agents good cover as they came in after the thugs.

"Another motel owner who's going to be mad at us for creating a disturbance," Shelley said as they pulled up at the office of a place called Pine Cabins.

"And he's picked such an imaginative name," Matt quipped.

She managed a small smile.

They checked in and left their luggage in the bedroom, then drove back to the shopping district which was filled with restaurants, art galleries, clothing stores and even some real estate offices.

"I don't see any sign of the FBI," Shelley whispered.

"That's the point," he answered. "They don't want to be

obvious. And they don't need to watch us to know where we are."

She glanced at him. "Let's hope Owens isn't double-crossing us."

He nodded. Indeed.

"So why do the bad guys think we're just walking around town like this?" Shelley asked.

"Because we lost them, and we assume we're safe."

"Are we really that stupid?"

"Okay. We're in town because you need warm underwear." He pointed toward an outfitter that sold cold-weather gear for both men and women.

Inside, Shelley tried on a thermal undershirt while Matt hung around the dressing rooms. It made him nervous to have her out of his sight, but he couldn't go into the booth with her.

She came out with the shirt in her hand.

"Does it fit all right?"

"Yes, but it's expensive, and I don't really need it," she said in a low voice.

"But we'll get it, because that will add realism to the shopping trip."

"I'm spending a lot of your money," she murmured as they stood in line at the cash register.

"Don't worry about it."

"I'll pay you back."

"Of course not!"

When they stepped onto the sidewalk again, he took her gloved hand in his and they started walking back toward the car.

He wanted to ask her a question, but he was having trouble summoning the words. Finally, he blurted, "If I had asked you to marry me, would you have said yes five years ago?"

He was surprised when she didn't give him an instant positive answer.

And his chest tightened as he waited for her to say something.

After half a minute, she murmured, "I'd have had to think about it."

"Why?"

She kept her gaze straight ahead. "Because you were obviously resisting the idea of marriage, so I would have worried that it wouldn't work out in the long run."

He wanted to argue that he had ached to marry her, but he'd thought he was doing the right thing.

He swallowed, because there was one more question torturing him. As they kept walking, he asked, "And what if I asked you to marry me now?"

This time, her answer came too fast. "I'd still have to think about it."

"Okay," he managed to say as he felt everything inside him squeeze painfully. He wanted to tell her that whatever happened, they belonged together, and that he'd been a fool to break off with her five years ago. But he knew she wasn't capable of hearing that now. He also knew she wasn't the same woman who had walked away from him. She'd been raising a child on her own and doing a very good job of it.

They continued down the street as though there was nothing unusual about the conversation. Still, he couldn't banish the terrible tension knotting up his stomach.

And he was sure it wasn't just from the personal conversation. He couldn't shake the conviction that the guys who had been following them around had found them again.

He wanted to stop and turn quickly to scan the cars in back of them. Instead, he forced himself to keep walking.

"IT'S THEM!" Don Campbell pointed to the couple on the sidewalk, just passing a mound of dirty snow piled along the curb. "Looks like they're having a heart-to-heart conversation."

He slowed the car, letting the couple get twenty yards ahead on the sidewalk. "Where the hell have they been?"

Savage shrugged. "We'll find out when we scoop them up."

"Suppose they've been somewhere…you know, important?"

"Like where?" Savage snapped. They'd taken this damn job without knowing all the background, and that was eating at him. He'd thought this gig was going to be easy, but the guy who'd hired them had put them in a dangerous situation. Savage would like to know how dangerous, but he wasn't in a position to demand answers. That could be dangerous, too. Now all he wanted to do was scoop up Whitlock and Young and deliver them to whoever was in charge, then get the hell back to Denver. And then figure out where they were going from there.

Campbell shrugged. "I'm just sayin'."

Savage gestured toward the bag Whitlock was carrying. "They've been shopping for warm clothes."

"Yeah." Campbell hung back, pretending he was looking for a parking space as Whitlock and Young crossed the street to a carryout restaurant and went inside.

"Looks like they think they're in the clear," Savage said.

"Can we get them out here?"

Campbell looked at the crowds on the sidewalk. "Too conspicuous. Let's see where they're going."

After ten minutes the couple came out again with another bag and walked down the block to one of the public parking lots that the town provided to make it easy for tourists to stop and shop.

They got into the same car they'd parked at the motel earlier and turned out of the lot.

Campbell followed at a discreet distance. When they turned in at a cabin court, he grinned and continued past the entrance.

"Cabins. I guess they're looking for privacy."

"I guess we're going to give them a nasty surprise."

THE MAN named Blue watched the sleeping boy for a few minutes, then closed the door and walked into the front room of the cabin.

It was time to make his report.

Pressing the speed dial, he waited for his contact on the other end of the line to pick up.

"How's it going?" the familiar voice asked.

"I've got the kid drugged and bedded down for the night."

"Good."

"So it's okay to take off the handcuff?"

"Yeah."

"Just make sure he's secured when he wakes up in the morning."

"Are you getting any effect from the treatment?"

Blue hesitated, trying to make an accurate evaluation. "I'm not seeing anything unusual."

There was a pause on the other end of the line. "Maybe he'll turn out to be a dud. Which means he does us no good. You get my meaning?" The harsh tone told him what he needed to know.

"Sure. I understand," Blue said, his own voice hesitant. He'd taken this job because he was committed to the project, but he hadn't considered the consequences of failures. He was prepared to kidnap kids and give them painful shots, not off them.

"Give it a few more days before you call it quits."

He breathed out a little sigh and looked toward the closed bedroom door.

"Okay."

MATT CLOSED the door to the room and leaned back against the barrier, glad to be off the street.

The gun he'd taken away from the man this morning was

in his luggage. He could get it out, but would that make it more likely that they'd get killed?

"You think they spotted us?" Shelley asked, breaking into his thoughts..

"I think there's a good chance."

"But you didn't see them?" she pressed.

"I couldn't identify anyone specific, but I wasn't looking because I didn't want them to think we knew we were in danger."

She made a small sound. "In danger."

He quickly revised the statement. "From their point of view. They think we're easy pickings because they don't know the FBI is in position here."

"We hope."

Ignoring the comment, Matt said, "Let's have a fire." After putting the food bags on the table, he knelt in front of the fireplace, which was already set with logs and kindling. All he had to do was strike a match and blow on the flame a little to get a good blaze going.

Shelley was sitting at the table, staring into space.

Glancing at her, he asked, "Are you hearing Trevor again?"

She shook her head. "I'm trying to reach him, but he's off the air again."

"That's what you call it?"

She nodded. "I guess we have to come up with a whole new vocabulary for the people with talents. Like your mom calling what you do 'giving a push.'"

"Yeah." Matt hesitated for a moment before asking, "Are you worried about Trevor? I mean, since we found out all that stuff from Jack and agent Owens."

"I'm always worried. But it's not worse than usual."

"Good." He dragged in a breath and let it out. "Let's try to act normal."

They opened the food, both of them staring at the fire as

they ate a little of the lasagna and marinated salad they'd bought.

He was too tense to taste anything, because he kept expecting a knock at the door. Instead, the seconds dragged by.

He thought of turning on the TV, but that would make it harder to hear anyone outside.

The wind had picked up, blowing the branches around. A scraping sound at the window made them both jump.

"Just pine branches," he said.

Shelley nodded and got up. Walking to the window, she stared out into the darkness.

"You think they want to kill us?" she asked in a voice she couldn't quite hold steady.

"I don't know."

"Great dinner-table conversation." She sat down and took another nibble of her lasagna. "What are they waiting for if they know we're here?"

"Maybe they're being cautious, since we screwed them up a couple of times."

"Three times."

There was no knock like the last time. One second the door was closed and locked. The next second, it was flung open and hung on bent hinges as a large man in a heavy coat and a ski cap charged into the room, bringing a wave of frigid air with him. It was the same man who had chased Shelley around the breakfast room. Apparently he'd replaced his gun, and he pointed his new weapon at Matt and Shelley.

Matt saw Shelley sink down in her chair as he turned to face the attacker.

"What the hell do you want?" he asked.

"Shut up. You're coming with us."

Us. So where was the other one? Waiting with the engine running to drive away as soon as his partner brought them out?

"Not likely," he answered, expecting the FBI to come charging in behind the thug. But as seconds ticked by and nobody else appeared in the doorway, the awful thought leaped into his mind that they were on their own.

Chapter Eleven

As Matt stared at the man with the gun, a raft of unwanted scenarios swirled in his head. Had Owens double-crossed them? Or hadn't the guys from the bureau gotten into position yet?

"Let's go," the big man growled. "This time we're not having any problems."

Matt glanced at Shelley, seeing the rigid lines of her face. Lord, he'd set this up, and now they were both in big trouble. But he wasn't going to let anything happen to her.

Scrambling for a plan, he said, "It's cold outside. Can we get our coats?"

The man hesitated, obviously torn between haste and practicality.

"You're not sending a lady out in a South Dakota winter in just her indoor clothes are you? Or were you planning to freeze her to death?" Matt asked.

"Okay, get your coats. And hurry up. We don't got all night."

Yeah, right.

The outerwear was lying over the arm of the chair. Matt wanted to tell Shelley to grab her coat and hit the floor before the shooting started. Instead, he clamped his teeth together because there was no way to warn her of what he had in mind.

He waited while she slipped into her jacket, then picked his up and moved closer to the thug as he pretended to pull the jacket over his shoulders. But instead of slipping his arms through the sleeves, he whipped the coat over his head and threw it at the man with the gun, hitting him in the head and covering his face.

An expletive roared from beneath the jacket as the guy made a mad scramble to unencumber himself. As his arms flailed, the gun went off, the shot zinging between Shelley and Matt.

He kicked out and caught the thug in the legs. The guy went down like a bag of horse feed dumped out of a truck.

He was flapping around on the floor still trying to free himself from the coat as Matt closed in to get the gun.

Before he could step on the guy's hand, three men pounded into the room.

Matt recognized Special Agent Owens in the lead, his timing off by a couple of minutes.

"FBI," Owens shouted. "You're surrounded. Toss out the gun—slowly."

He motioned Matt and Shelley out of the way, and they both stepped back.

When the man on the floor hesitated, Owens ordered, "Do it, if you don't want to get hurt."

The guy slid the gun across the floor, and an agent rushed forward to get it. Another pulled the coat off the thug and cuffed his hands behind his back.

"Where the hell were you?" Matt asked in a dangerously calm voice.

Owens glared at him. "Outside. We saw the car pull up, but they have the interior light turned off. We didn't see this guy open the door and slip out."

Yeah, great, Matt thought, but he kept his mouth shut because he didn't see much advantage in pointing out that the Bureau had screwed up this operation.

"You've got his friend?" he asked instead.

"Yeah."

He couldn't stop himself from saying, "Lucky we didn't get drilled."

Owens was ready with an accusation of his own. "If you had, it would have been your own damn fault," he shot back as another agent hustled the thug out of the room. "What the hell were you trying to do with that coat?"

"Since you didn't show up, I was trying to keep the guy from herding us into the car. Next time, don't leave me thinking that we're on our own," Matt suggested.

Without bothering to answer, Owens turned away. "We'll be in touch."

"Wait a minute, I want to know who these guys are working for."

"When we find out, we'll let you know," the agent answered.

"How will we get in contact?"

"We'll call you."

"Before you go, I want you to come to the office with me and tell the manager that the door got broken by an FBI operation."

"Not likely. We're keeping a low profile." Turning, Owens disappeared into the night, leaving Matt and Shelley staring at each other.

"What are we going to do?" she gasped looking from him to the door and back again.

He'd been too busy to register the cold air pouring into the room.

"We're not staying here." Matt started gathering up the possessions they'd left in the room. "Once again, the motel doesn't have our real names. I guess we're going to disappear into the night and leave some money to pay for the door."

"We didn't break it."

"But I guess you could say it's our fault."

"More likely, the FBI's. They should have arrested the guy before he got this far. Arrest," she murmured, her eyes narrowing. "I didn't hear them read him his rights."

Matt nodded, realizing Shelley was correct. "Maybe they're going to claim Homeland Security issues, and just stash those guys away without anybody knowing about it."

She winced. "I don't like that—even for them."

"Yeah, but right now, I think it's the best thing for Trevor. We don't want the man holding him to know that anything has gone wrong with their operation."

While Matt wrapped up the food, Shelley insisted on leaving a note apologizing for the door and saying that someone had come in to rob them. He told her to print it in block letters, so that her writing would be less recognizable

"The management is going to wonder why we didn't stick around to talk to the cops. Or maybe not. I guess we're leaving a trail all over the Rapid City area. The local fuzz probably think we're Bonnie and Clyde," she added. "Sorry."

"You don't have to apologize. We're both on edge."

Matt turned off the lights and the heat, and they both stepped outside where he pulled the door against the frame as best he could.

Shelley gave it a regretful look before they both hurried to the car. Moments later, they pulled out of the parking spot in front of the cabin and headed for the highway.

Feeling like a fugitive, he turned left and drove toward the outskirts of town.

Shelley sat beside him, her hands rigid in her lap.

"Are you hearing anything from Trevor?" Matt asked.

"No," she clipped out, and he stopped trying to make what passed for conversation in this situation.

When the motels became fewer and farther between, he slowed down at one with a vacancy sign.

"Okay?" he asked.

"Whatever."

Before going in, he looked at the clerk through the lighted window, giving him some silent instructions. *Don't worry about these people. They're just passing through the area, and you'll forget about them as soon as you finish registering them.*

Hoping that would do the trick, he signed them in under a false name again. If they were lucky, the break-in hadn't made the evening news, and his description wasn't being broadcast on the police frequencies.

In the room, Matt kicked off his boots and coat, then flopped onto one of the two beds.

Shelley glanced at him, and he knew she was deciding whether to join him. He wasn't surprised when she pulled back the covers on the other bed.

Apparently, they weren't going to be cuddling together tonight, and he wasn't going to say anything about it. Any level of intimacy was her decision, although he couldn't hold back a stab of pain. He needed the comfort she could give him. Apparently, she wanted to distance herself from him.

He closed his eyes but kept them slightly open, watching her move about the room.

He'd lain down in his clothing. She rummaged in her bag for a clean shirt and jeans, then disappeared into the bathroom. Moments later, he heard the shower and couldn't stop himself from imagining her naked under the running water.

If he went in there and stepped into the shower with her, would she be angry? Maybe not. But he wasn't going to press her now. Not when she'd made it clear that their relationship was totally up in the air.

After she came out and slipped into the other bed, he got up and took his own bag into the bathroom, where he showered and changed.

When he came out, she was lying with her eyes closed, but

he doubted that she was sleeping. Probably she was sending out messages to Trevor.

He was too tense to relax. So much had happened in the past twenty-four hours that he couldn't process it all. The attack this morning. The horrifying trip to the Facility. The bargain with Owens and the near disaster of the assault. Could all that be crammed into one horrendous day?

He guessed it had to be, unless his brain was completely scrambled.

Finally fatigue got the better of his churning mind, and he fell into a dreamless sleep.

A hand on his shoulder had him ready to fight off an attack, but when his eyes blinked open, he found himself staring into Shelley's face.

"What? Is something wrong?"

"No. Trevor's on the air again."

He sat up. "Okay."

Her eyes clouded. "At first he sounded groggy, like they'd drugged him. Maybe that's how that guy Blue gets some sleep. He makes sure Trevor is out."

"The bastard."

"But then his voice got stronger."

"Good." He wanted to pull Shelley down onto the bed with him and hold her tight—just for a little while. Just for a little strength and comfort. But he kept his hands at his sides.

Her expression held a mixture of triumph and regret. "I think that, you know, the treatments are making a difference. He's able to talk to me more loudly."

He sat up, still forcing himself not to reach for her. The look on her face told him that she was concentrating hard. He thought Trevor must be talking to her, and he wanted to ask what his son was saying, but he didn't interrupt.

She sat very still for long moments. Finally, she made a little sighing sound.

"What?"

"He says Blue was asking him questions. Asking if he felt any different or if he could do anything he couldn't do before."

Matt caught his breath. "What did he say?"

"He said he was just the same."

"Okay. Good."

"Maybe."

He stared at her. "What does that mean?"

"Blue's questions were pretty urgent. I think he was anxious to have Trevor tell him he could do something...extraordinary."

"If he does, Blue will know we're in contact with him."

"Yes," she whispered. "But..."

"What?"

"What if...what if they...they give you the treatment, and if you don't respond, they..."

Her voice trailed off, but he could follow her thinking process, because that terrible possibility had been in his mind since they'd toured the Facility.

Still, denial leaped to his lips. "No!"

"To save his life, he might have to tell Blue what he can do, and then we'll never find him!"

Matt couldn't hold back a curse.

She gave Matt a pleading look. "Will you let me try that thing I wanted to do?" she asked, her voice high and strained.

"Which thing?"

"Let me try to find him—using the contact we have. I think that if we start driving, I can zero in on him." She licked her lips. "I told him I was coming to get him."

"Yeah. I think we'd better do it."

"Thank you," she breathed.

"But you're going to have to tell him it's not just *you*. It's *us*."

"I'll wait until we get closer."

He ached for her to tell Trevor that his daddy was riding to the rescue, but he wasn't going to press the point now.

"We should leave," Shelley said.

"And grab some breakfast on the way," he said, because he had to keep thinking of the practical situation.

They both started moving around the room, throwing the things they'd taken out back into their travel bags.

When he was packed, he started for the door to the room, then decided to look out the window first.

The sight outside stopped him dead. A police car was parked in front of the office.

Shelley must have seen his shoulders stiffen. "What?"

"The police," he answered, silently cursing their luck.

He saw her panic. "Are they looking for us?"

Knowing he had to be honest with her, he answered, "That's a good possibility. We're probably famous by now. I mean, our fifteen minutes of fame—at least in Rapid City, South Dakota.

"What are we going to do?"

"When I checked in, I gave the clerk a push, and I didn't say there were two of us. Maybe the cop won't know we're here. Or what he's looking for, exactly."

"We left our fingerprints in the other room," Shelley breathed. "If they compare them to ours—they've got us."

He made an angry sound, watching as the cop came out of the office and stood looking speculatively at the row of rooms. So much for giving the clerk a push. They should have gotten out of here before the shift change in the morning. Or maybe it didn't matter. The patrol officer was going to do his thing, regardless.

Matt followed his gaze, seeing that there were eight cars still in front of the row of fifteen rooms.

As they watched, the lawman started across the parking area toward the rooms.

"Now what?" Shelley whispered.

He thought for a moment. "You go out, get in the car, and drive away. Since I didn't register you, you're probably somebody else's wife, or a woman treveling alone."

"Then what?"

"Head toward town. We've got phones now. Wait until I call you that the coast is clear."

When she looked like she was going to panic, he reached for her and pulled her close, feeling her tremble in his arms. It was amazing to him that she was still functioning after everything that had happened, but she was too strong and determined to give up.

"All I want to do is get my son back," she whispered.

"I know. And we will. Make sure your phone is on."

Shelley reached into her purse, pulled out the phone and turned it on.

"Don't worry about the cop. Just walk outside like you're minding your own business, get in the car and drive away."

She clutched him more tightly for a moment, then sighed and moved away.

When she started to pick up her bag, he stopped her. "Wait. Don't take any luggage. That way it will look like you're just going to get something to eat."

"What are you going to do?"

"Stay in here with the door closed. Or maybe try the bathroom window trick."

"And then what?"

"Make for the woods." And leave a trail in the snow again, he thought, but he didn't say it.

She nodded, and stepped toward the door, where she dragged in a breath and let it out before reaching for the knob.

He kept the slat on the shade up just enough so that he could see outside.

Shelley stepped out the door and started walking at a moderate pace to the car. Counting the seconds as they passed,

Matt thought she was home free until the lawman turned and started walking toward her.

She ignored him until he called out to her. "Ma'am. Just a moment, ma'am."

Chapter Twelve

With what she hoped was an open but questioning look on her face, Shelley turned toward the cop. He was a young guy, about her age, dressed in cold-weather gear.

"Yes, Officer? Is something wrong?"

"Just doing some checking. Can I see some identification?"

She froze, wondering if Matt could hear what was going on.

"Checking on what?"

"Can I see some identification?" he said again.

"Of course," she answered, reminding herself that her driver's license wasn't going to incriminate her. As far as the authorities knew, nobody by the name of Shelley Young had been making mischief in the Rapid City, South Dakota. area. Of course, nobody named Shelley Young was going to match the registration for the motel room, either.

Or the registration on the rental car, she thought as she realized that only Matt's name was on the contract. Which meant that technically she wasn't supposed to be driving the car. If he asked to see the contract, she was in trouble.

She waited with her heart thumping while the young officer looked at her license.

"You're from Colorado. What are you doing up here?"

"Unwinding," she said with a smile. "I have a high-stress job, and I had to get away for a few days."

"I know what you mean."

"This is the perfect place to have some winter fun," she said conversationally, trying not think about how much *fun* she was really having—like playing hide and seek with an armed thug in the breakfast room. Or having the same guy break down the motel room door. Or what about a winter car chase?

Mommy?

The cop caught the startled look on her face.

"Ma'am?"

Thinking quickly, she said, "Did I just see a moose in the woods over there?"

He turned and scanned the trees.

I'm talking to a police officer, honey, Shelley said without speaking. *I need to finish with him.*

Okay.

"We do have them, but not usually this close to town," the officer said.

"I'll keep my camera ready."

As the cop handed back the license and tipped his hat to her, she slowly eased out the breath she'd been holding.

Before he could ask any more questions, she unlocked the car and climbed in. Seconds later, she was driving out of the motel parking lot and heading toward Rapid City with her heart pounding so hard that she thought it might break through the wall of her chest.

Mommy?

I'm right here.

You were frightened.

I didn't want the policeman to know I'm looking for you.

Why not?

Because it has to be a secret.

He was silent for a few moments, and she was afraid that she'd lost contact with him. Then he said, *Okay. Are you going to be here soon?*

As soon as I can.
I don't like it here. I don't like Blue.
I know, honey. I know. Mommy's coming for you.
I want to go home.
I know! she answered, her heart squeezing.

A horn honked and she realized that she had been sitting at a red light that had turned green.

Starting up with a jerk, she kept going toward town, then pulled into the drive-up line at a fast-food restaurant where she bought two breakfast sandwiches and two cups of coffee. But once again, she didn't know what to do. Was Matt okay back at the motel?

THERE WAS no window in the bathroom. Matt hadn't noticed that detail the night before.

Now he was trapped in this room.

He looked at the luggage, debating whether to try and take it. It would weigh him down a little, but if he left it in the room, he'd be advertising that a man and a woman had stayed here last night. And the cop had only seen a woman come out. So he'd know something funny was going on.

With a sigh, he picked up the bags and listened to the cop knocking on doors, then opened his own door a crack and looked out.

While the officer was talking to someone halfway down the line of rooms, Matt grasped the straps of both bags, picked up the luggage and stepped out, walking at a normal pace toward the office.

As he'd suspected, the clerk behind the counter wasn't the same one he'd seen before. Last night's had been a man. This was a young, redheaded woman. The brass nametag on her gray suit said her name was Janet.

"Help you?" she asked.

"My wife had to go into town. She'll be picking me up in

a while," he said. With every ounce of persuasive power he possessed, he sent her a silent message. *I need a place to wait for her. I can't wait in the room. I hurt my leg, I can't stand up for long periods of time. You need to let me stay in the office until she comes back.* Turning, he looked through the window. The cop was moving along the line of rooms in the opposite direction, but would he come back to the office when he was finished or would he drive on to the next motel?

"Is there someplace I can wait?" he asked out loud, keeping his voice even.

"We don't usually allow guests in the back, but I can make an exception for you, seeing as you hurt your leg and all," Janet answered.

For a moment she looked confused, and he sent her a reinforcement message, telling her the story all over again.

"Thanks so much. I really am grateful."

"Come around this way."

She gestured toward the end of the counter, and raised a section that was on hinges so he could come through. Then she opened a door to an office with a computer sitting on a desk with a chair in front. He dropped into the chair as though his leg was paining him.

"I won't be any trouble," he said, hoping it was true, considering his last several motel encounters.

When Janet went back to her post, he breathed out a sigh and glanced around the room. There was only one way in and out, so he was trapped if something happened.

Well, he'd talked his way in here. Maybe if he had to, he could talk his way out. How long did he have to wait for the damn cop to leave? And which way was the guy headed? Had he started in town and worked his way out here? Or was it the other way around? And how many more officers were looking for the couple who had gotten into a fight with someone in one motel and wrecked another?

Wondering what was happening outside the office, he glanced at the door. Maybe he'd gotten himself into more of a trap than a hiding place.

Feeling too exposed in the chair, he got up and started poking around. First he stowed the two travel bags in the bottom of the supply cabinet. Then he began looking for someplace to hide. There was a narrow space between the back of the desk and the wall. It was too skinny for him to squeeze into, but after he moved the desk forward a few inches, he was able to slip behind it, press his back against the wall, and stretch out his legs. The modesty panel at the back of the desk hid him.

Glancing toward the door, he sent Janet another message. *There's nobody in the office. There's nobody in the office.*

Would she believe it? He guessed he'd find out.

With his head resting against the wall, he closed his eyes, remembering that a few days ago, his life had been normal.

Or it had seemed that way. He just hadn't found out yet about Dr. Sykes, the Facility and his own strange background.

It was hot, and he unbuttoned his coat. Still, he couldn't help feeling the room was closing in around him. At least there wasn't a bright light shining on him.

After a while, his legs started to fall asleep. He was thinking about moving when the door opened.

"See, nobody here," the woman named Janet said.

He breathed shallowly as he waited to find out what would happen.

"Yeah, Thanks."

It was probably the cop who'd stopped Shelley.

They stood in the doorway for several moments, and he heard the clerk say, "Everybody's talking about this crazy man and woman who have been making trouble in town. They already trashed a couple of motels."

Oh, great, Matt thought.

"Yeah," the officer answered.

Janet lowered her voice. "I heard they escaped from a mental institution."

Even better, Matt silently added.

"We don't know that, ma'am."

"But you didn't find them yet?"

"We will."

"Or they're out of the area."

Yeah, they're out of the area, Matt agreed, this time sending the message to Janet and the cop. Maybe they'd take the hint.

Still, Matt braced for the officer to look behind the desk and find him.

After what seemed like several lifetimes, the door closed again.

Matt shut his eyes, catching his breath. He had to get out of here. But not until the lawman left the motel.

Ordering himself to stay calm, he waited for several minutes, then pulled his phone out of his pocket and dialed Shelley. When she didn't answer immediately, his chest tightened. Then she finally clicked on.

"Where are you?" she asked.

"Hiding behind the desk in the motel office. The cop checked in here, but he didn't find me."

"Good."

"Where are you?"

"Heading back—with breakfast."

"There may be more cops looking for us. Apparently there's a rumor going around town that we escaped from a mental institution."

She made a gagging sound. "I guess that's as good an interpretation as any."

"If the patrol car is still in the parking lot, keep driving by. If it's gone, pull up to the main entrance and call me."

"Okay."

She signed off, and he put the phone on vibrate, then waited where he was, hoping nothing else was going to happen before she got there.

Of course, it didn't work out that way.

Someone pulled open the door and paused for long moments. Then he heard an annoyed male voice call out, "Janet."

"Yes, sir?"

"Who moved the desk?"

"Is it moved?"

"Of course. Just look at that." The man strode forward. When he reached the desk, he made a startled sound as he caught sight of Matt.

His only option was to rise, fling himself out of the cramped space and knock the guy over.

The man landed on his behind, and Matt charged out of the office, abandoning the bags that he'd stowed in the storage cabinet.

Janet stared at him in shock as he leaped past her.

Forget about me. You never saw me, he broadcast, wondering if the message was getting through.

Dashing outside, he ran across the parking lot. Shelley hadn't arrived yet.

Oh, great.

Grimly, he sprinted into the woods, staying parallel with the road. How far away was the cop? Would he be back in seconds or minutes?

Dividing his attention between the motel and the road, Matt saw the manager come out and look around.

Matt kept moving, hoping the trees hid his location. Finally, after an eternity, he saw Shelley coming.

He stepped out of the trees, waving frantically at her, and she headed for him. Snatching open the car's back door, he climbed inside and wedged himself onto the floor.

"Drive," he ordered. "They're looking for a man and a woman. If we're lucky, they didn't see you."

"I think they did."

"Perfect." He sighed. "The manager discovered me, and I had to leave the luggage in the motel office. Was there anything in there that would connect your bag to Shelley Young?"

"I hope not." She thought for a moment. "It was an old bag and I didn't have a luggage tag on it."

"Good."

"What should we do now?"

"Get the hell out of town as fast as we can."

"And go get Trevor."

"You know where he is?"

"I've been talking to him. I think I can find him. I think if we turn left at that intersection up there, we'll be heading in the right direction."

"We have to make sure we're safe first."

"We have to get him!"

"Shelley, think. If we get caught, *nobody* will be able to rescue him."

She made a sound that was a cross between a curse and a moan. "Then what should we do?"

"Did you pass anything like a general store on the way here?"

"Yes."

"Stop in there. Buy some electrical tape and a pair of scissors, if you can get them."

She kept driving, and he wondered if she was following his directions. Then she turned off the highway and into a parking lot.

"Park away from other vehicles so nobody can look in and see me. Then get in and out of there as fast as you can."

"Okay." She climbed out of the car, and he stayed out of sight on the floor.

A few minutes later, she was back with the items he had requested. "Now what?"

"Try to find an out-of-the-way place where I can fool with the license plates."

She kept going for several miles, then turned into another parking area. Peering up above the window level, he saw that they were in a gas station that was closed.

"Drive around back."

She continued on to the rear of the building and turned around so that she was facing the road.

"Give me the tape and the scissors."

After she handed him the bag, he climbed out into the cold, squatting to look at the rear license plate. As he'd remembered, it had several numbers and letters, one of which was an L, which he could change into an E with the tape.

With his gloves off, he unwrapped the tape, then cut a strip, which he pressed onto the license plate in a horizontal line at the top of the L. Then he cut another strip to fill in the middle of the E. Standing back he looked at his handwork and decided it would do, if nobody gave it too close an inspection. Satisfied, he repeated the process with the license plate on the front of the car.

When he was finished, he turned toward Shelley and saw her staring into space.

"Are you talking to Trevor?" he asked when he climbed into the back seat again and sat down on the floor.

"Yes." She drove off, heading toward the edge of town. "Are you going to stay in back?"

"I'd better stay out of sight until we get away from the Rapid City area. Or are we leaving this area?"

"I'm not sure."

"You can't say how far we're going?"

"No."

He reached between the seats and took the bag with the

coffee. It was completely cold, but he drank it anyway and ate the cold breakfast sandwich that Shelley had brought for him.

"We have enough gas?" he asked.

"Maybe we'd better stop."

"Then I guess I need to get into the trunk—so nobody will see me."

She winced. "I hate that idea."

"So do I, but I think it's necessary. At this point, we're better off having people think you're alone.

They pulled into the parking lot of a shopping center.

"Let's throw away the trash—so it doesn't look like you had two breakfasts."

"You think of everything."

"I'm trying. When you open the trunk, you could be putting your purchases inside."

"Right."

After getting rid of the breakfast rubbish, she parked between two vans which hid the car from view. When she'd opened the trunk he got out, checked to see if anyone was watching, then climbed quickly into the rear compartment.

"I'll let you out as soon as I can," she said as she enclosed him in darkness.

He knew he'd suggested this ploy, but he had to fight a wave of panic as he tried to get comfortable in the cold, confined space. First he'd wedged himself behind a desk. Now this.

Shelley pulled out of the parking space. When she slammed on the brakes, he cursed under his breath, even though he knew she hadn't done it on purpose.

As she kept driving, he thought about calling her on the phone because it would help to hear her voice. Then he decided that would only startle her to have the phone ring, and he didn't know the laws in South Dakota about talking on a cell phone while you were driving.

The trunk gave him no protection against the South Dakota

cold, and he pulled up his knees and hugged them, fighting to keep his teeth from chattering. When he'd come up with this brilliant plan, he hadn't realized that he was going to turn into a Popsicle.

He'd thought he'd been uncomfortable behind the desk. This was ten times worse. But at least he could move his legs around as the car rolled down the highway.

"Isn't there a damn gas station anywhere around here?" he muttered.

When Shelley finally pulled off the highway, he would have cheered, if he hadn't needed to remain silent.

Instead he waited while she crept forward, then stopped again, and he imagined that she had pulled up at one of the pumps.

He heard her pop the lid then unscrew the gas cap. Finally, gas began to flow into the tank.

She'd be finished soon, and they could get out of here. Then she'd find a quiet place where he could climb out of the trunk and get back into the front seat where he'd be sitting close to the heat vents.

She was screwing the gas cap back on when he heard a voice say, "Hey lady, you've got a problem with your license plate."

Chapter Thirteen

After a long pause, Matt heard Shelley say, "Oh, damn! I got it last week, and I guess it must be defective or something."

"Let me take a look. I think one of your letters is peeling off."

Matt fought not to start screaming.

"No thanks!" Shelley answered. "My husband is expecting me home soon." She waited a beat to emphasize the point. "He'll take care of it."

The guy stopped talking, probably because Shelley had told him she was married. Still, Matt waited with his breath frozen in his lungs, then felt the car shift as she climbed back inside and slammed the door. In seconds, she was roaring out of the station and down the highway.

He imagined the guy who'd offered to help staring after her, wondering about her behavior.

Hopefully, he wasn't anyone official or the kind of guy who liked to call the cops. If they were lucky, he was just a man who wanted to help a pretty woman, and had found out she was already taken.

Don't speed. He cautioned her. *You don't want a patrol car to stop you.* He added, *Sorry. The license plate mess is my fault. I thought I was being so clever with that trick. I guess the cold made the tape peel off.*

He held out a small bit of hope that she could answer him, but heard nothing. He waited with his breath shallow in his lungs for the sound of a siren behind them. If an officer saw the black strips peeling off the license plate, he was going to be suspicious.

But the car kept moving at a steady pace down the highway, and finally, she slowed and made a right turn. After driving for another minute, she cut the engine. Quick steps came around to the back of the car, and the trunk opened.

Sitting up, he blinked in the light.

"Are you all right?" Shelley asked.

He moved stiff arms and legs.

She watched him with a sympathetic look on her face. "You must be half-frozen."

"I'm okay."

Fighting the numb feeling in his extremities, he slung a leg over the side, then climbed out, bracing his hands against the lower lip of the trunk. Relieved to be free again, and fighting not to sway on his feet, he looked around and saw only trees on either side of them.

"Where are we?"

"The driveway of a farm or a ranch. You can't see the house from here—or the road. I could tell from the look of the tracks in the snow, there's only been a little traffic. So they probably don't come in and out much."

"Good thinking."

"I hate dodging the authorities like this."

"I know," he answered, reaching for her.

She came into his arms, holding on fiercely and they clung together.

He'd vowed not to start anything between them, but he couldn't stop himself from lowering his mouth to hers for a passionate kiss. Her lips moved under his, just as urgently, and he took what she offered, greedy for the taste of her.

Needing more, he unzipped his coat, then hers, so that he could pull the upper part of her body against his, sealing them together with heat. His hand came up between them, cupping her breast through her shirt, and she made a small sound that might have been protest—or passion.

He was pretty sure what would have happened if they'd been in a motel room. But out here on this road, they both knew they were safe from going too far. So he indulged his craving for her for a few more moments, kissing her and touching her, and letting her know how much he wanted her. When they finally broke apart, his head was swimming.

She rested her cheek on his shoulder, her breathing ragged. He had never wanted her more, but he knew that anything personal between them must wait until they had accomplished their mission and gotten their son back.

"You did good," he murmured as he brought his own breathing under control.

"I was scared."

"I know. So was I."

"Lord. Is it ever going to end?"

"Yes. It's going to end well," he said, punching out the words, because a good ending was the only one he would allow after everything that had happened. "And I understand now that it's going to take the two of us. I mean, neither one of us can do it alone."

"I think you're right."

She held him for another half minute before making a snorting sound and saying, "Where did you get that nutball idea of putting tape on the license plate?"

He gave her an apologetic look. "From a suspense novel. It worked for the hero."

She laughed. "Yeah, well, the guy in the novel probably wasn't driving around in below-freezing weather."

"I guess you're right." He eased away from her, then pulled the tape off the back plate while she did the front.

"I'll drive," he said.

She climbed into the passenger seat, and he slid behind the wheel.

"Too bad you don't have that baseball cap."

"Yeah. Or anything else we brought. Like the gun."

"That was in the bag?"

"Unfortunately. I guess it's only a matter of time before the cops find it."

"It will have your fingerprints."

"Maybe they're not on record anywhere. And it won't just be mine. The thug's are there, too."

She was silent again, then shifted in her seat. "When you were in the trunk, I heard you."

"You mean you felt the push—when I told you not to speed."

"Yes, but I also heard you talking to me in my head, telling me you were sorry about the tape. It was like the way I can hear Trevor."

He turned in surprise to look at her then back at the road.

"Did you get any...replies from me?" she asked.

"Sorry. No."

"Well, I guess it's just one way."

"Or you're honing your receiving talents," he suggested

She didn't answer, and when he saw her look of concentration, he whispered, "You're talking to Trevor?"

"Yes."

"What's he doing?"

"Having lunch. Peanut butter and jelly."

"Okay. That's normal. And no else is there with them?"

"He's never mentioned anyone else." Still, she asked if Trevor was alone with Blue and got an affirmative answer.

They came to a crossroads, and he slowed. "Which way?"

She pointed toward the left. "There."

He turned left, and they kept going, the road hemmed in by the pine forests and the rock formations that were so much a part of the area. The surface had been plowed, but not recently, and he kept coming to icy patches.

He ached to go faster, but he had to keep testing the pavement to make sure they weren't going to go sliding off into the woods.

He was thankful that they had a full tank and also thankful that there were few other drivers on the road. Especially patrol cars. Apparently the authorities weren't going too far afield to look for the weird couple.

They kept driving, not saying much, and he knew Shelley was speaking to Trevor. Occasionally she'd say something out loud.

"We're getting close, honey," she murmured.

"Tell him he can't give you away," Matt cautioned. "He has to make sure Blue doesn't know anybody's figured out where they are."

"Trevor, make sure Blue doesn't catch on that I'm coming to get you." Then she stopped talking out loud, and he felt left out of the conversation.

He kept his gaze on her for a few seconds, then dragged his attention back to the road. There was so much he wanted to say to her. About the past. About the present. And especially about the future. But he couldn't interfere with her silent communication. Instead, he just kept driving, praying that she could guide him to their son.

The landscape was empty of almost everything except trees and rock formations jutting out of the pines. As they traveled into the back country, they saw few houses, although now and then he caught a glimpse of smoke rising from the chimney of cabin in the trees. There were roads leading off to the left and right. Some of them were marked by signs like Hurley's Retreat. Or The Jacksons. But some were totally anonymous. Unfortunately, the roads had become progressively narrower and the paving worse.

A couple of times, the tires sank into potholes that were hidden by the snow.

Matt felt his tension mounting and knew it was worse for Shelley, because this rescue operation depended on her knowing *where* they were going. Well, not where in the normal sense. They had no directions—only her sense that she was getting closer to Trevor.

He glanced at her again, then brought his eyes back to the road. Each second that ticked by felt like an eternity. He wanted to ask for another reading, but he managed to keep from distracting her, because he knew it wouldn't help either one of them.

After what felt like an eternity, she spoke.

"We're close."

"How close?

She turned her hand palm upward. "I can't say exactly. I'll know it when I see it. I guess." When they came to a crossroad, she said, "Turn left here."

He followed her directions, wondering if he was going to be able to get back to civilization once they picked up Trevor.

They had traveled another two miles when she made a small sound.

"What's wrong?" he asked, worried that she had lost the connection—or worse, that she was seeing a scene of disaster.

She looked as if she was going to be sick. "This is the wrong way."

"You're sure?"

"Yes!"

She'd told him where to turn, but now she sounded anguished and apologetic, all at the same time.

"I said turn around!" she shouted, and he knew that she was at the end of her emotional rope.

"I have to find somewhere wide enough."

She sat rigidly beside him until he came to a place where the shoulder widened out. Cautiously he backed off the road, then came forward again, trying to make sure they didn't get stuck in the snow.

When he glanced at Shelley, he saw she had her hands clenched in her lap so hard that the knuckles were white.

He couldn't stop himself from asking, "What happened?"

"I'm not sure. I just got mixed up. Maybe because we're so close."

"Okay."

"I'm sorry!"

"I know you're doing the best you can."

She dragged in a breath and let it out. "So are you, but we're both pretty strung out."

They traveled back the way they'd come. "Go the other way," she said, pointing down a narrow side road that he hadn't seen before.

The road surface was gravel, and he had to slow down to stay on it.

Finally they came to a long driveway that wound into the pine forest. It wasn't marked by a sign like some of the other lanes they'd seen, and there were no tracks going in and out.

"Stop!" Shelley shouted, her voice ringing inside the confines of the vehicle, and he came down hard on the brake, making the car skid. He held his breath, praying they wouldn't plow into a tree.

She pointed up the gravel roadway. "He's there. Not far."

"You're sure?"

"Yes!"

She'd been wrong before, but his only option was to rely on her ability to zero in on Trevor.

He wanted to ask how she was doing it, but he thought she probably couldn't explain it. Just the way he couldn't explain the mechanism for giving people a push.

When he started the car again, then pulled off into a small clearing, she made a shocked exclamation and grabbed his arm, her fingers digging through the padding of his jacket. "What are you doing? We have to go get him."

Trying to keep his voice even, he said, "We can't just drive up there. Think about it. That guy Blue is probably armed. What's going to happen when he sees a car coming up the road?"

She pressed her lips together, then looked at him. "You're right. I'm not thinking this through. What should we do?"

"Get out and walk. But not along the road." He cleared his throat. "I think it's time to tell him that you're not alone. Tell Trevor his dad is with you."

She reached for his hand and pressed her palm down in a gesture he knew was meant to comfort.

"I know this is hard on you. I understand you want him to know you're here. But won't that be too big a shock? I mean, we're trying to keep him…quiet."

Matt considered her assessment. He ached to let Trevor know that his dad was there with his mom, but he saw the wisdom of keeping his identity under wraps for a while longer.

"Okay. Tell him you've got a man with you—a friend. Somebody who's here to help."

She sat for a moment, silently communicating with her son.

"What does he say?" Matt asked.

"He understands. He says he'll act normal." She made a harsh sound. "If you can call any of this normal."

"It will be over soon," Matt soothed.

"Yes, but he's scared. It's almost time for another shot. And they hurt."

Matt clenched his fists. He wanted to tell Trevor that they'd be there before Blue hurt him again, but he didn't know if it was the truth.

Silently, they both pulled their gloves back on and climbed out of the car, then both started walking back along the road, before angling into the woods.

Luckily the snow wasn't too deep, and they could make fairly rapid progress through the pine forest.

"Can you control Blue?" Shelley whispered as they tramped through the trees.

"I can't influence a person I haven't seen. Which means we have to get right up to the cabin. Or I do."

"So do I," she whispered, and he knew there was no way he was going to keep her from her son.

They both kept silent, but when he glanced at Shelley, he saw that she looked as though she wanted to scream.

Finally, through the trees, they caught sight of a small building made of logs. Plumes of smoke came from a stone chimney protruding from the shingled roof.

They corrected their course, heading for the structure.

When they reached the edge of the trees, Matt stopped and studied the area. The setting looked quiet and peaceful. It could be one of the vacation retreats they'd passed, except that a thirty-yard wide swath around the cabin had been cleared of trees and brush. Why do that to a cabin in the woods unless you want to make sure nobody could sneak up on you?

Were there alarms, too? Matt hoped not. And so far, the odds were against it, because nothing in the woods had called attention to them.

He hoped.

Off to the far side of the cabin was another building. The door was open and he could see a four-wheel drive vehicle parked inside.

There were no tracks in the snow, which meant that nobody had been in or out of here since the driver had arrived.

As Matt peered out from his hiding spot, he evaluated their chances of making it across the clearing. And he had something else to worry about. Shelley had been wrong before. What if they were closing in on the wrong place?

"You're sure this is it?" he whispered.

She gave him a ferocious look. "Yes. I know he's in that cabin. He's just thirty yards from us."

"Okay," he answered, looking across the cleared space. "We'd better go in low so Blue won't see us if he happens to glance out the window."

It had started to snow—large, dry flakes drifting down from the sky as they stood among the trees.

They both dropped to the snow-covered ground and began belly-crawling across the open area, commando-style. It was hard slogging, with snow working its way up Matt's jacket and making his shirt cold and wet. He was glad that they only had to go thirty yards.

The snow created another problem. Twisting around to look behind them, he saw two trails along the ground, like giant snakes slithering toward their prey.

He hoped the guy inside wasn't going to look out and see the tracks.

When Matt glanced at Shelley, he saw her teeth were clenched, but he knew that she would crawl across ground glass or live coals to get to her son.

Halfway across the open space, she made a moaning sound. He wanted to ask what she was hearing, but he couldn't risk speaking out loud.

Could he send a silent question?

It might work, but it would only use up energy that they didn't have.

When they finally made it across the thirty yards, Matt sat up with his back braced against the wall of the cabin and shook the snow from under his jacket. Shelley did the same.

The flakes continued to fall, obscuring their vision as they stared back at the woods.

At least it was going to cover the tracks they'd made as they crossed the clearing.

Leaning toward her, he put his mouth against her ear. "What happened?"

"He's getting ready to give Trevor a shot." She went rigid.

"What's wrong?"

"I can hear Blue talking."

Matt pressed his ear against the side of the cabin and heard the man speak.

"You're sure you're not lying to me, kid?"

"Nooo," Trevor answered in a quavery voice.

"If you can't do something special, I'm gonna have to punish you."

Matt saw Shelley holding her breath, waiting for Trevor to confess that he'd been lying for days. But he said nothing.

"Nothing? You can't move things with your mind?"

"No."

"You can't talk to people who aren't here?"

"No!" Trevor said, his voice rising in alarm.

"You're sure?"

Matt cursed under his breath. Knowing they had to hurry, he stood, bending to keep most of his face below the level of the window. Shelley did the same.

It took a moment to realize what he was seeing. Then the picture came into focus.

A big man dressed in a plaid shirt was leaning over a little boy who was stretched out on a kitchen table. The man had a hypodermic in his hand.

Shelley gasped.

The man whirled toward the window.

At first Matt could tell that the snow obscured his vision. Then his gaze zeroed in on them, and a look of shock and anger bloomed on his face.

Chapter Fourteen

Inside the cabin, Trevor cried out and twisted toward the window, his face flooding with relief when he saw his mother staring in at him."

"Mommy! You found me, Mommy!"

The man's curse was loud enough to penetrate the glass. Dropping the hypodermic, he pulled a gun from the waistband of his shirt and pointed it at them.

Trevor gasped and flailed out his arm, catching the man on the shoulder.

"Get the hell off me," the kidnapper shouted.

"I hate you. You get away from me."

Matt watched in horror, praying that Trevor wasn't going to get hurt.

With desperate intensity, he focused on the man named Blue, sending him a message. *Put down the gun. Back away from the boy. Back up until you hit the wall across the room. Put down the gun. Back away from the boy.*

The man stared at him, obviously aware of the psychic order, but he didn't move, and he kept the weapon aimed at them.

Don't shoot. Put down the gun. Back away from the boy, Matt ordered, using every ounce of mental power that he had acquired since his kidnapping.

From the corner of his vision, he could see Shelley's tense

features. She must know that he was trying to give Blue a push and that it wasn't working very well. This man must have been trained to resist a psychic suggestion. Or he possessed psychic powers himself. Maybe he knew how to shield his mind so that no one could penetrate the barrier.

Was he one of Dr. Sykes's subjects? Someone who had joined the doctor's team?

There was no way to figure out the man's background—unless they asked him, and Matt was pretty sure they weren't going to have a heart-to-heart anytime soon.

Could he disable the guy and get him to talk?

Maybe, but first things first. They had to get Trevor.

Staring at his quarry, Matt redoubled his efforts, pouring out more power, although he wasn't sure what that meant.

When the man started slowly backing up, Matt sighed in relief, but the gun was still firmly in the kidnapper's hand. And Trevor was still on the table between the weapon and the window.

Put down the gun. You don't want to shoot anybody. Put down the gun and keep backing away from the boy.

To Matt's vast relief, it seemed to be working.

Maybe his powers were stronger than the man's after all.

"Open the door," he told Shelley. "Then call to Trevor. Get him to come to you. Bring him outside."

"He needs a coat, or he'll freeze out here."

"Can you send him a message—tell him to get it?"

"Yes."

As he watched, Trevor gave a small nod, then slipped off the table.

"Stay here," Blue growled.

"I don't like you," Trevor answered. "I want my mommy."

"You have to stay with me."

"No! I won't."

A look of comprehension bloomed on the man's face. "Have you been talking to your mommy?"

Trevor lifted his chin, and this time his answer was a defiant, "Yes!"

"You little brat." The man gave Trevor a murderous look, then must have realized that he should be paying attention to Matt, not the boy.

"How did you find me?" he demanded, his gaze fixed on Matt.

"Trade secret."

"I don't think it was you." As he spoke, he tried again to wrench free and succeeded in raising his hand, reaching toward Trevor.

Stay away from the boy. Leave the boy alone. Put the gun down and back up. Press your arms against the wall.

Blue followed orders, his face a mask of anger.

Seeing his chance to get away, Trevor dodged around the man and ran into the bedroom. He was back almost at once carrying his coat.

"Go get him. Hurry," Matt said to Shelley between gritted teeth. "Then take him back to the car and get out of here while I hold the guy off."

Shelley gasped as she took in the implications. "What about you?"

Matt felt his insides squeeze. "I've got to stay here. Otherwise they guy is going to go after you and Trevor."

"No!"

"Do it. I'll give you as much lead time as I can. Drive to the police."

As he spoke, he saw the man raise the gun, and he switched his attention away from Shelley toward Blue, repeating his previous orders.

When he could speak aloud again he said to Shelley, "Go on. I love you. I got you and Trevor into this mess. I'm going to get you out."

Shelley made a moaning sound. "Matt, I love you. I can't leave you."

"You have to save our son. That's what's important."

She moaned again, then pulled open the door and dashed into the cabin. Scooping up her boy, she held him tightly against her chest, then eased away so that she could pull on his coat.

Seconds later, she was outside carrying Trevor.

Matt saw the man's gaze swing from him to the fleeing woman and child.

"Nooo! Come back, you bitch. You don't know what you're doing."

As Blue roared his protest, Matt felt the kidnapper make a superhuman effort to wrench away from the mental vise that kept him in place.

Matt hadn't expected that kind of resistance, and it took all of his power to keep the guy from breaking free and lunging toward Trevor.

"Go!" he shouted to Shelley.

She gave him an agonized look.

"Go, before it's too late."

After another second's hesitation, she started running with Trevor back the way they'd come.

Trevor was crying and calling "Mommy. Mommy."

SHELLEY CLUTCHED her son to her breast, fighting not to cry. She'd come to Matt because he'd been her only hope of getting Trevor back. And he'd done it. He'd done it!

Now he was sending her away, and she knew that if she left him here, he was going to lose the battle. Sooner or later he wouldn't be able to hold the kidnapper at bay.

A cry of anger and frustration rose from the depths of her soul.

"Mommy, what's wrong, Mommy?"

"It's all right."

"Who is that man, the one who came with you?"

"He's your daddy."

The boy gasped. "My daddy?"

"Oh, honey."

All she could do was keep running through the woods, back toward the car.

MATT DASHED from the window to the open doorway where he had a better line of sight to the kidnapper, determined to hold the bastard in place as long as he could.

Long enough for Shelley and Trevor to get away. He was pretty sure he wasn't going to survive this encounter. Eventually the man would fight off the mental compulsion. Then he'd start shooting.

Could Matt run into the woods and hide before that happened? Maybe, but he'd leave a trail of prints in the snow, just like the ones they'd made on the way up here.

Seconds ticked by, as he and the man faced each other. The mental struggle wasn't something anyone could see, but Matt could feel the silent fight.

The two opponents glared at each other.

To Matt's shock, the man spoke. "I'll get you."

"I'll take that chance," he answered. "What do you want with my son?"

"He's an important part of a research project."

"The hell he is."

It was hard to keep up the conversation and keep his attention on fixing the man in place. Maybe that was the kidnapper's objective—to distract Matt.

It looked as though it was working, because the man took a step forward.

Matt redoubled his efforts, praying he was giving Shelley and Trevor enough time to get away.

The seconds dragged by, and Matt wondered how long he could keep up this desperate struggle.

Then, in the distance he heard a noise that made the hairs on the back of his neck prickle.

Lord, no!

He prayed that he was wrong, but moments later, he saw the rental car come skidding up the driveway.

"Get out of here!" he shouted as Shelley pulled to a stop in back of him.

She rolled down the window. "Get in!"

He wanted to refuse, but he had no option now. She was here, and if they didn't get away, they were both going to die.

He waited for one more minute, giving the man a blast of psychic energy that would have fried the brain of a normal human being. But Blue was hardly normal. He just stood there looking at Matt with hate-filled eyes.

Whirling away, Matt jumped into the front passenger seat of the rental car.

Trevor crouched in the back, wide-eyed as Shelley tried to turn around, her tires skidding on the snow-covered road.

As she struggled to maneuver them out of the area in front of the cabin, Matt kept his gaze on Blue, willing him to stay where he was. And willing him not to raise his gun.

After an eternity, Shelley got the car turned in the right direction, then started down the access road. Matt kept his gaze fixed on Blue, who slowly seemed to come out of a trance, shaking his head as he stared after them.

"Hey. Come back."

He ran to the open cabin door, shooting at them while they made tracks down the driveway. As far as Matt could tell, none of the bullets hit.

He wanted to shout at Shelley that she was a fool for coming back. The purpose of this mission was to rescue Trevor, and she'd gotten what she came for.

But maybe she heard him inside her head, because she spared him a glance as she made her way back to the public road.

"I couldn't leave you."

He wanted to say they might all end up dead, but he kept the thought to himself—he hoped—because now was not the time to make things worse.

Behind them he heard an engine roar, and he knew that Blue had run to his car and started the vehicle. He wasn't going to let them get away without trying to recover the boy.

As they turned right onto the highway, he glanced behind him, seeing the SUV barreling down the narrow track behind them.

"I tried to call the police," Shelley said as she kept driving. "But I couldn't get a signal."

"Of course not. They've been chasing us around for days, but when we need them, they're unavailable."

Shelley increased their speed as the other car turned onto the road and came after them.

When she started to skid, she eased up on the gas pedal again, and he wished he were behind the wheel because he had more experience driving in the snow, but they couldn't stop to change drivers.

Matt kept his gaze in back of them, seeing a hand reach out the window of the other car. Then a hail of bullets came flying toward them.

Hoping against hope, he pulled out his own cell phone and dialed 911. But like Shelley, he got no signal. They were too far out in the wilderness for their phones to work.

All they could do was keep driving as the man pursued them.

Trevor's gaze fixed on Matt. "Mommy said you're my daddy."

"Yes."

"I never had a daddy."

"You always had a daddy. I just didn't know about you."

"Why not?"

"Your mom and I had an unfortunate miscommunication."

"What's a miscommunication?"

"We'll talk about it later—when we have more time," he said, wishing he knew how to be a good father. He'd been focused on rescuing Trevor, but he hadn't thought much past that. Not in practical terms.

His own mom had been a lousy parent, and he knew he didn't want to repeat her mistakes. But he hadn't gotten much beyond that conviction.

His thoughts were rudely interrupted by another blast of gunfire. Apparently the man had gotten close enough to them again to think he had a good chance of stopping them.

"Mommy!"

"It's okay, honey. Everything's okay," Shelley said in a soothing voice as she kept going.

"But he's shooting at us. Like on TV."

"We'll get away."

Shelley kept driving, her gaze fixed straight ahead, until she made a gagging sound.

Fear leaped inside Matt. "What is it? Are you hit."

"No. But he must have gotten the gas tank. The gauge is going down to zero. What should I do?"

Matt craned his neck, looking in all directions. In back of them, the other car was catching up.

At least they hadn't burst into flames, like on TV, he thought. That was something.

Off to the right, through the trees he could see one of the rock formations coming up. "Maybe we can hide from him in those rocks. Pull off the road. As soon as you stop, start running. I'll grab Trevor."

Shelley pulled to the side of the road. "You'll be right behind me?" she demanded.

"Of course. I'll have Trevor."

She took off toward the rocks, and he opened the back door, snatched up his little boy, and followed Shelley into the woods.

The snow was falling harder now, making it almost impossible to see where they were going. But the towering rocks were a landmark they could use.

Clasping Trevor in his arms, he kept running, hearing the breath hissing in and out of his lungs.

The boy ducked his head, resting it against Matt's shoulder.

Matt couldn't spare a glance behind him, but he heard another shot ring out.

Only one. The guy must be conserving his ammunition. Was he running out, or did he just need to reload?

Through the snow, Matt could just make out Shelley ahead of him, moving as fast as she could.

When she stumbled, he caught up with her, pulling her up by the arm and steadying her on her feet.

"Mommy, I'm scared," Trevor whimpered.

"We're okay," Shelley answered automatically, and Matt prayed that it was true.

Ahead of him again, Shelley stopped and gasped. Matt caught up with her. "What?"

She pointed. "This formation must be a plateau. There's a drop-off up ahead. I would have fallen over it I'd kept going."

"Okay." He peered through the snow and saw a place to the right where natural spires stuck up. "Get behind there. Hold Trevor tight." He swallowed. "Cover his head."

As he handed her their child, she gasped out, "What are you doing now?"

"I'm solving our problem," he said, glancing back toward the precipice.

A look of comprehension bloomed on her face. Holding Trevor tightly, she disappeared behind the barrier.

Matt watched them go, thankful that they were shielded.

But he didn't want the guy going into the rocks and looking for them. Crouching low, he veered away from Shelley's tracks, running along the edge of the cliff. The ground was treacherous, and he could barely see. When he slipped and almost went over the edge, he slowed down, placing his feet more carefully, hoping Blue wouldn't see the danger until it was too late. Matt kept expecting the guy to start firing again. When he didn't, it was further proof that the bastard was out of ammunition.

Or was it just too chancy to take a shot in this storm?

Matt moved farther from the two people he wanted to protect most, hoping he wasn't going to come to a place where the cliff curved inward—because then he was the one who would go over the edge.

Looking up, he saw Blue was closing in, and he knew it was time to make his stand before the guy realized that the land dropped off sharply just a few feet behind Matt.

Stopping in the snow, he turned and stood with his back to the precipice, then took a dozen steps forward, waited for the man to spot him.

Come on. Come and get me. You can get me. You just have to keep coming after me.

This time there was no resistance to the push, Blue came charging out of the blinding snow, looked around and spotted Matt.

"Who are you?" he shouted as the guy rushed forward.

"You'll never find out."

"You kidnapped my son. Don't you owe me an explanation?"

"I don't owe you squat."

So much for conversation, Matt thought, switching back to silent communication.

Come get me. Come on. You can get me, Matt chanted over and over.

Then he turned and ran toward the drop-off.

He heard Blue panting behind him. Praying that his desperate plan was going to work, he pretended to keep running through the blizzard, raising and lowering his legs as he reached the edge of the cliff.

Chapter Fifteen

As Matt heard Blue close in on him, he dodged to the side. Running too fast to change course, the other man kept hurtling forward, over the edge of the cliff. He tumbled off into space, disappearing into a swirl of snow.

His scream echoed up from far below.

Long seconds passed during which Matt was frozen in place. Then he moved away from the cliff edge and started back toward the rocks where he'd left Shelley and Trevor.

As he approached, she emerged from behind the barrier holding their son.

"Is he gone?" she asked in a shaky voice.

"Yes. He won't bother us again," Matt said, his gaze meeting Shelley's

When she answered, "Thank God," he felt some of the tension in his chest ease.

"What are we going to do now?"

"We're going home. Back to the ranch. When we get there, we'll talk about our next move," he added, because he knew nothing was settled between them. Not yet.

They tramped back through the blinding snow, and Matt was thankful that he could see their footprints, otherwise he knew they could easily get turned around.

They reached the road, and he saw the bullet-riddled car that they'd been driving.

The other vehicle was pulled in behind it.

"We've got to take his car."

"I don't want to."

"Yeah. But we don't have a choice."

When he reached the other car, he pulled open the driver's door.

"Lucky the keys are in the ignition," he told Shelley.

They all climbed inside. Shelley sat in back with Trevor. Matt turned the ignition to get the heater going.

Like Shelley, he hated using Blue's wheels, but he didn't see any alternative. They weren't going to get anywhere in a vehicle with holes in the gas tank.

"What are we going to tell the rental company?" she asked.

"That we ran into some nut who started shooting at us," he replied. "That's the truth."

"Yeah!" Trevor said, finally finding his voice.

Matt looked over his shoulder. "Everybody okay?"

"Yes," Shelley answered.

Trevor's gaze was fixed on him. "Are you really my daddy?" he asked.

A wealth of emotions welled up from the depths of Matt's soul. He had been so intent on finding this little boy, and now they were only a few feet away. He swallowed hard. "Yes, I am. And I'm really glad to have you in my life." He glanced at Shelley, still unsure of where she stood.

"Where were you?" Trevor demanded.

"I was at my ranch. I didn't know about you. But I was really happy to find out."

The boy continued to stare at him. "Are we going to live with you now?"

"I hope so."

Shelley shifted Trevor on her lap. "How do you feel?" she asked.

"Good. Now."

She glanced at Matt, then back to her son. "Did you get a lot of shots?"

He shrugged. "Some."

Matt broke into the conversation. "I want to get back to Colorado."

"Yes," she answered.

At least he was thankful they agreed on that. He hoped the rest of it would fall into place. He pulled away from the shoulder and turned the car around, heading back toward Rapid City.

There was so much to talk about, but this wasn't the best place. Still, there was something he needed to say.

"Probably you shouldn't tell people that you can talk to your mommy—" he fumbled around for a way to put it and came up with "—through the air."

"I know," Trevor said in a low voice. "It makes me weird doesn't it?"

"No. It makes you special. But we should keep it a secret. Okay?"

"Okay," the boy agreed.

Matt had gotten only a few miles when he saw a car coming up behind him—fast. As it approached, blue and red lights began to flash.

He cursed under his breath. "It's the cops."

Another unmarked police car joined the first one and edged them over to the shoulder.

Matt pulled over and cut the engine.

"Mommy," Trevor whispered.

"It's okay," Shelley murmured. "We haven't done anything wrong."

Matt wondered if the cops would see it that way.

Four officers approached them, guns drawn.

"Out of the car! Hands where we can see them."

Knowing it could be fatal to argue, Matt did as he was told.

Another officer approached the back door and motioned to Shelley and Trevor to get out.

"Down on the ground. On your bellies."

"Please, no," Shelley gasped.

"Down on the ground."

Matt and Shelley both got down on the frozen ground, and Trevor started to cry.

"Leave my mommy alone."

When he started hitting one of the officers, the man turned and held on to him.

Another one patted Matt down, then cuffed his hands behind his back. They also cuffed Shelley. And another officer searched the car.

"What's this about?" Matt demanded.

"You're the man and woman who've been making trouble at motels all over Rapid City."

"Not us," Matt said.

"You have the right to remain silent…" one of the officers began.

"We haven't done anything. Our son was kidnapped, and we were rescuing him," Shelley cried out.

The officer turned to Trevor. "You were kidnapped?" he asked.

"Yes!"

"And who are these people?"

"My mommy and daddy," Trevor sobbed out. "Don't hurt my mommy and daddy."

"Who kidnapped you, son?"

"A man named Blue."

"Where is he?"

"I don't know. He disappeared in the snow. I think he was running after my daddy."

An officer hauled Matt to his feet. Another man pulled Shelley up. "We'll straighten this out."

Matt raised his head. "If you go back up the road a few miles, I can show you our car. It's riddled with bullets from Blue shooting at us. He hit the gas tank. We're lucky our car didn't explode. This is his SUV."

"You mean you stole a car?"

"You're not listening to me."

"Come along, son," one of the cops said to Trevor.

"No! I want my mommy."

"You can see your mommy later."

"No, please," Shelley cried out. "He was kidnapped. We just got him back. Let him ride with me."

When they still looked doubtful, Matt realized that in the heat of the moment, he'd forgotten he had an advantage. Silently, he began to speak to the men again

Don't hurt Shelley and Trevor. Let the boy ride with his mom. He repeated that several times, then added, *You know I'm telling the truth. We're innocent victims. It wasn't us who trashed those motels. It was the bad guys trying to stop us from finding our son. The FBI has them in custody.* He repeated the message several times, then began to speak aloud.

"Call FBI Special Agent Perry Owens. He'll vouch for us," Matt said aloud.

"We'll do that," one of the officers said.

"Let my son ride with his mom."

The officer relented. "All right."

At least he'd accomplished something. Still, they were being treated as suspects. The cops put Matt into the back of one car and Shelley and Trevor in another.

"Matt," Shelley cried out.

"It's okay," he shouted back. "It will be okay." As he said it, he was praying it was true.

When the car with Shelley and Trevor drove away, he turned to the officers who had him in custody.

Go back the way we came. At least look at our car. You'll see he riddled it with bullets.

Then he said it aloud. "Go back the way we came. At least take a look at our car."

The men hesitated, and Matt used the silent push again.

To his relief, the officer turned the unmarked around. When they came to the rental car pulled onto the shoulder, they stopped, and the officer got out.

"Bullet holes, all right," he reported to his partner, then turned to Matt. "You're lucky the gas tank didn't explode."

"Yeah."

"What happened to the shooter?"

Matt dragged in a breath and let it out, then gestured with his head. "See those tracks? That's where we climbed out of the car and made a run for it. The guy followed us, still shooting. There's a drop-off about a hundred yards ahead. It was snowing so hard that he couldn't see where he was going. He went over."

"And we won't find out he was shot when we recover the body."

Matt kept his gaze steady. "That's right. We were unarmed."

"Because you left your gun in that motel office."

Matt shrugged. "Not my gun. It belonged to one of the men who was chasing us."

"Uh-huh."

The man turned away and started toward the rocks. Matt and one of the officers waited in the car.

The cop who had gone to investigate was back fifteen minutes later.

"I can see where it happened," he said.

"Then uncuff me."

"Not until we find out why you trashed a bunch of motels."

"Like I said, it wasn't us. It was the men following us around."

"What is this—a conspiracy against you?"

"Something like that. We can stop at the cabin where Blue was holding my son."

"I think we've had enough side trips for the moment."

Matt could have pushed the guy. But he knew they would get to the kidnap hideout sooner or later. Instead, he took another tack

"Like I told you, we've been working with the FBI. With agent Perry Owens who's been out here on a special assignment. If you contact him, he'll vouch for what's happened." *I hope,* Matt added under his breath.

"If so, they haven't been operating according to regulations."

Matt shrugged. "Ask Owens about it."

As they drove into town, he tried to get comfortable with his hands cuffed behind his back.

"What happens to my son?" he asked.

"They'll take him to child protective services—unless you have a relative in the area."

"We're from Colorado."

"Then juvenile services will take him and give him a medical check-up."

"God no! He'll be scared out of his mind. We just got him back, and he needs his mother."

"Sorry," the officer said, sounding sympathetic. "But we can't bend the rules."

"Of course not," Matt muttered, and it wouldn't do any good to push these guys. They weren't the ones who had Trevor.

They drove back to Rapid City, to the police headquarters. Inside the building, Matt looked around for Shelley and Trevor, but he didn't see either one of them.

"Call Special Agent Perry Owens," he said again, praying that the cops could find the guy—and that he'd cooperate. For good measure, he said it silently, too.

But instead of answering, they hustled him into a cell, and when the door clanked closed behind him, he had to fight the urge to scream. Another cell. Like years ago. Only different, he told himself as he sat down on the hard bunk, ordering himself not to freak out.

Time dragged. He tried to reach out to Shelley, but he had no sense that she was even in the building. Maybe it had something to do with the construction. Or maybe there was a limit to his power, and he was just so burned out that he couldn't use it now.

That thought wasn't comforting.

Instead he lay on his bunk trying to keep from leaping up and shaking the bars of his cell.

Finally footsteps came down the hall. When he looked up, relief washed over him. Perry Owens was with one of the officers who had taken them into custody.

"You vouch for him?" the officer said.

"Yes. We were running a sting operation, trying to get the kid back. Only Whitlock and Young panicked and took off after the boy on their own."

That wasn't exactly what Matt remembered, but he wasn't going to contradict Owens, since the guy had come down here.

The officer unlocked the cell and took them to a lounge area, where Matt's heart leapt when he saw Shelley and Trevor on a plastic couch.

"Thank God," he said, rushing toward them. He wanted to pull Shelley into his arms, but she was holding Trevor, who had fallen asleep, probably from exhaustion. Instead he sat down next to her and slung his arm around her shoulder.

The cops and Owens must have worked something out, because the officer left, and the FBI agent sat down on a couch opposite them.

"What about the guys who were following us?" Matt said.

"They're not talking."

"Great."

"But we have their cell phone records. We think they are working for Sykes—or the Association. It's just a matter of time."

"I hope so."

"I'd like to have a look at the cabin where Blue was holding your son."

"Okay." He looked at Shelley. "I can take Special Agent Owens back there. Why don't you and Trevor wait for me here in town?"

She hesitated a moment, and he knew she was torn. She didn't want to be alone, but at the same time, she didn't want Trevor anywhere near that place. Finally she nodded.

Matt turned to Owens. "Get her a room in a five-star hotel. The FBI can pay for it."

The agent gave him an annoyed look. "It's not enough that I got them to drop all charges against you?"

"That's right."

Owens sighed. "Only for one night."

They drove to a resort hotel, where Matt settled Shelley and Trevor into an expensive suite.

Once they were back in the car, Owens said, "I see you were smart enough not to mention Sykes's experiments. I'd like to keep that information quiet."

"How do we do that?"

"We act like this was a kidnapping—for ransom."

"If you say so."

"You want to expose your kid to a media circus and have the world think he's a psychic freak?"

"No," Matt snapped.

"Okay. I've already persuaded the cops to keep this under wraps. They think other children will be in jeopardy if this story gets out."

"Clever."

"For all I know, it's true."

Matt nodded.

"You just have to follow my lead."

They returned to police headquarters where they picked up one of the officers who had arrested Matt and Shelley. Then Matt, Owens and the cop drove back to the cabin.

"They were holding your son for ransom?" the cop asked.

"Yeah," Matt answered because he'd decided that Owens's plan made sense.

"How did you find him?"

"A tip."

Inside the cabin, the cop looked at the hypodermic lying on the floor. "What's this, drug paraphernalia?"

"Maybe the guy was a drug addict," Owens said, and Matt knew that the agent had already thought of the answers he was going to give. Probably a clean-up team was on it's way to take away the evidence the FBI wanted to remain hidden.

When Matt saw the small handcuff attached to the bedpost, he almost lost it. But he managed to keep his cool because he knew he had to.

"You're satisfied this is a kidnap scene?" Owens asked.

"Yes," the officer answered.

"Then I'm sure Mr. Whitlock would like to get back to Ms. Young and their child."

The cop nodded, and they climbed back into the car.

"I appreciate your discretion," Owens said when they dropped the cop off back at the station.

Finally, Owens drove to the hotel. "I'd like to talk to Trevor," he said.

"Not now."

"I thought that was part of the deal."

"I'm taking him back to the ranch. After he has a chance to unwind, you can talk to him."

"Did he acquire any special powers?" Owens asked.

Matt hesitated, then finally said, "He was able to reach out to his mother. That's how we found him."

Owens whistled through his teeth.

"He's just a little boy, and he's been traumatized. He needs to mend."

"You're sure your lady will go back home with you?"

Matt looked down. "I'm hoping she will."

"We'll keep the ranch under surveillance," Owens said. "Sykes isn't going to get to you again."

Matt nodded. But he wasn't going to let down his own guard.

He hurried up to the suite and found Shelley and Trevor in the sitting area, sharing a room-service meal of hamburgers and French fries.

Shelley gave him a questioning look.

"Everything's fine," he said.

She pointed to a plate with a metal dome. "Your burger and fries are under there. I think they should be warm."

He sat down on the couch and took the cover off the plate, staring down at the simple meal.

"The fries are good," Trevor said.

Matt picked one up and chewed. "You're right."

Trevor watched him eat. "You're really my dad?" he asked again.

"Yes," he answered, struggling not to choke up.

"My mom's been telling me about you. You live on a ranch, and you used to have horses."

"I'm going to have them again," he said, because he could see that part of his future very clearly, even if he couldn't see the rest. Giving up the profession he loved had been part of his withdrawal from the world. Now he was determined to plunge back in—no matter what.

"And Mom says you have an airplane."

"That's right."

"Can I fly in it?"

"Tomorrow. I'll take you back to the ranch."

"Cool! Are we going to live with you now?"

Matt swallowed. "I want you to. If that's what your mom wants."

He held his breath, waiting for her answer.

"Yes."

"Thank the Lord." He reached for her and pulled her into his arms, holding tight.

"Are you gonna do a lot of hugging?" Trevor asked.

"Yes," they both said.

Matt fought the tears stinging the backs of his eyes. In a thousand years, he never would have imagined this moment.

"Can I hug, too?" Trevor asked.

"Of course." Matt held out his arm, and the boy launched himself against him. He gathered his son close, holding the two people who mattered most to him in the world.

After a while, Shelley eased away. "You need to finish your dinner, then it's bath time."

"There's nothing for my bedtime story."

"What stories do you like?" Matt asked with a lump in his throat.

"Green Eggs and Ham."

Shelley laughed. "That's no problem. We both know that one by heart."

"We don't have the pictures."

"We'll tell your dad what the pictures are."

"Okay."

Matt sat in the big bathroom while Shelley bathed their son. And he sat with them in bed while they told him the green-eggs-and-ham story.

There were a few difficult moments at the end where Trevor didn't want to go to sleep. But Shelley was firm.

They both kissed Trevor good night, then slipped into the living room.

"You're a good mother," Matt said.

"I try to be."

"It must have been hard for you."

"I understand now that I made it harder than I should have. I should have come back to you with Trevor."

"You're here now."

"I was terrified that you'd be angry with me."

"I'm thankful that I have the two of you now."

"What's going to happen?" she whispered. "I mean about Sykes?"

"The FBI is going to keep a watch on us."

"Good. But I wish they didn't have to talk to Trevor."

"I know. But we owe them something—for helping us."

"Because it was to their advantage," she reminded him.

"But we're going to live our lives like normal people. All three of us."

"If we can."

He gave her a fierce look. "One thing I learned over the past few days is that I want everything I've missed. As a kid. And with you and Trevor."

"Won't it be expensive to start working the ranch again?"

"Yeah, but some of my horses are at a neighboring spread. Ted Dunster boarded them for me. And as soon as I tell people I'm back in business, they'll come to me."

"And I can help out. I mean, I don't have to give up my clients. I do most of my work by e-mail anyway. That will bring in a decent income."

"Yes. But enough business talk."

He lowered his mouth to her for a long hungry kiss, and when he finally came up for air, his head was spinning.

"Oh, my," he said. "That's different."

"How?"

"I don't have to feel guilty about wanting you."

"Oh, Matt. Oh," she said again as his hands moved urgently up and down her back, then cupped her hips, pressing her against his erection.

He was about to start unbuttoning her blouse, when a small voice said from the doorway, "Are you going to get married?"

Shelley jumped and eased away, but he managed to keep his cool. "Yes we are," he said.

"Can I come to the wedding?" Trevor said.

"Of course. You can be my best man."

"What does that mean?"

"The man who stands beside the groom and hands him the wedding ring."

"Okay."

"What are you doing out of bed?" Shelley asked.

"I just wanted to make sure you were getting married."

"Nothing to worry about on that score," Matt answered.

Shelley took one of her son's hands and Matt took the other and they walked him back to his bed, where they tucked him in again before heading to the other bedroom, where Matt locked the door and turned to Shelley.

"That could have been embarrassing."

"You'll have to get used to having a little pitcher with big ears—and eyes—around."

"Not a problem."

He gathered her close and brought them back to the place where they'd been before they were interrupted.

"I love you," he said, between passionate kisses. "I never should have sent you away."

"I always loved you. I shouldn't have left."

"Oh, Lord, Shelley. I'm never going to let you go. Neither one of you."

"And I'll be at the ranch. With you. Where I should have been all along. I'm sorry it took something bad to send me back to you."

"But you're here now. That's what counts."

"Yes," she murmured against his lips as they proclaimed in no uncertain terms what they meant to each other. Now and forever.

* * * * *

Don't miss the next book in the
MAXIMUM MEN *series,*
INDESTRUCTIBLE by Cassie Miles,
on sale in March 2010 wherever
Harlequin Intrigue books are sold!

*Rancher Ramsey Westmoreland's temporary
cook is way too attractive for his liking.
Little does he know Chloe Burton came to his
ranch with another agenda entirely....*

That man across the street had to be, without a doubt, the most
handsome man she'd ever seen.

Chloe Burton's pulse beat rhythmically as he stopped to talk
to another man in front of a feed store. He was tall, dark and
every inch of sexy—from his Stetson to the well-worn leather
boots on his feet. And from the way his jeans and Western shirt
fit his broad muscular shoulders, it was quite obvious he had
everything it took to separate the men from the boys. The
combination was enough to corrupt any woman's mind and
had her weakening even from a distance. Her body felt flushed.
It was hot. Unsettled.

Over the past year the only male who had gotten her time
and attention had been the e-mail. That was simply pathetic, especially since now she was practically drooling simply at the
sight of a man. Even his stance—both hands in his jeans pockets,
legs braced apart, was a pose she would carry to her dreams.

And he was smiling, evidently enjoying the conversation
being exchanged. He had dimples, incredibly sexy dimples in
not one but both cheeks.

"What are you staring at, Clo?"

Chloe nearly jumped. She'd forgotten she had a lunch date.
She glanced over the table at her best friend from college,
Lucia Conyers.

"Take a look at that man across the street in the blue shirt,
Lucia. Will he not be perfect for Denver's first issue of *Simply*

Irresistible or what?" Chloe asked with so much excitement she almost couldn't stand it.

She was the owner of *Simply Irresistible*, a magazine for today's up-and-coming woman. Their once-a-year Irresistible Man cover, which highlighted a man the magazine felt deserved the honor, had increased sales enough for Chloe to open a Denver office.

When Lucia didn't say anything but kept staring, Chloe's smile widened. "Well?"

Lucia glanced across the booth at her. "Since you asked, I'll tell you what I see. One of the Westmorelands—Ramsey Westmoreland. And yes, he'd be perfect for the cover, but he won't do it."

Chloe raised a brow. "He'd get paid for his services, of course."

Lucia laughed and shook her head. "Getting paid won't be the issue, Clo—Ramsey is one of the wealthiest sheep ranchers in this part of Colorado. But everyone knows what a private person he is. Trust me—he won't do it."

Chloe couldn't help but smile. The man was the epitome of what she was looking for in a magazine cover and she was determined that whatever it took, he would be it.

"Umm, I don't like that look on your face, Chloe. I've seen it before and know exactly what it means."

She watched as Ramsey Westmoreland entered the store with a swagger that made her almost breathless. She *would* be seeing him again.

* * * * *

Look for Silhouette Desire's
HOT WESTMORELAND NIGHTS by Brenda Jackson,
available March 9 wherever books are sold.

Devastating, dark-hearted and...
looking for brides.

Look for

BOUGHT:
DESTITUTE YET DEFIANT

by *Sarah Morgan*

#2902

From the lowliest slums to Millionaire's Row...
these men have everything now but their brides—
and they'll settle for nothing less than the best!

Available March 2010
from Harlequin Presents!

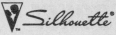

ROMANTIC

SUSPENSE

Sparked by Danger, Fueled by Passion.

Introducing a brand-new miniseries
Lawmen of Black Rock

Peyton Wilkerson's life shatters when her
four-month-old daughter, Lilly, vanishes.
But handsome sheriff Tom Grayson is
determined to put the pieces together and
reunite her with her baby. Will Tom be able
to protect Peyton and Lilly while fighting
his own growing feelings?

Find out in
His Case, Her Baby
by
CARLA CASSIDY

Available in March wherever books are sold

LARGER-PRINT BOOKS!

GET 2 FREE LARGER-PRINT NOVELS

◆ HARLEQUIN®

INTRIGUE®

PLUS 2 FREE GIFTS!

Breathtaking Romantic Suspense

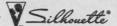

SPECIAL EDITION

FROM *USA TODAY* BESTSELLING AUTHOR
CHRISTINE RIMMER

A BRIDE FOR JERICHO BRAVO

Marnie Jones had long ago buried her wild-child
impulses and opted to be "safe," romantically
speaking. But one look at born rebel Jericho Bravo
and she began to wonder if her thrill-seeking side
was about to be revived. Because if ever there was
a man worth taking a chance on, there he was,
right within her grasp....

*Available in March
wherever books are sold.*

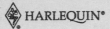

HARLEQUIN®

INTRIGUE

COMING NEXT MONTH

Available March 9, 2010

#1191 KILLER BODY
Bodyguard of the Month
Elle James

#1192 RAWHIDE RANGER
The Silver Star of Texas: Comanche Creek
Rita Herron

#1193 INDESTRUCTIBLE
Maximum Men
Cassie Miles

#1194 COLBY JUSTICE
Colby Agency: Under Siege
Debra Webb

#1195 COWBOY DELIRIUM
Special Ops Texas + Colts Run Cross
Joanna Wayne

#1196 UNDER THE GUN
Thriller
HelenKay Dimon